Protocol X

Neutrinoman & Lightningirl
A Love Story

Episode #3

Robert J. McCarter

Little Hummingbird Publishing
Flagstaff, AZ

Published by:
Little Hummingbird Publishing
P.O. Box 23518
Flagstaff, AZ 86002
www.LittleHummingbird.com

Little Hummingbird Publishing is a division of Arapas, Inc. Find more about Arapas at: www.Arapas.com.

For all those who believe love is the greatest superpower!

Chapter 1

One Foot in Front of the Other
Late Winter 2005, Superstition Mountains, Arizona

MY FEET THUDDED ON THE DIRT TRAIL BELOW ME, DRY and dusty. I was trail running in the Superstition Mountains east of Phoenix, but the Sonoran Desert surroundings were pretty much lost to me. I was focusing on one foot at a time, one breath at a time, and had attention for little else.

Endurance training. Actually my life since the "Incident at Yellowstone" (as it was commonly called) had become one big training session. A crashed alien spaceship, corpses of aliens, and working alien energy weapons had changed things.

And Licia, she had changed things too.

One foot in front of the other, one breath at a time.

Even as tired as my body was, even as focused as I had to be, I couldn't keep the thoughts of Licia out of my mind. I hadn't seen her in six weeks. Colonel Williams had decided to train us separately for a while. I had to wonder if that wasn't by her request, because it certainly wasn't what I wanted. I figured I was being paranoid, but given what I had experienced in the last few months I was becoming a staunch believer in paranoia—in fact, I think as a q-morph it is a job requirement.

And if I never saw her, how was I going to get her back? This training was taking up nearly all my time. They had even dispensed with the pretense of me working as a janitor at Palo Verde Nuclear Generating Station. I was busy with them all day, every day. I had tried calling her and texting her that first week after she had broken it off. But she didn't answer, and she didn't return my messages.

One foot in front of the other, one breath at a time.

The military had decided that I needed to do endurance training. I ran cross-country for a few years in high school, so running it was. The trail running had been my idea. I wasn't going to run circles on some damn military base. I wanted to get out into the desert. Let nature do its work, let it take some of this tension away.

Well, tension isn't the right word. Trauma is. And they had me seeing a therapist for that. I really preferred running and sweating in the beauty of the Arizona desert to sitting in a room with my torturer—err, therapist—talking about how I felt about killing the aliens. Did they think that I wasn't supposed to be traumatized? Did they think I could go through all that and come away with a laugh and a smile?

It's just not that simple.

These thoughts, Licia, trauma, and the aliens, kept floating up in my mind. And the running and breathing chased them out. My runs were getting longer and longer, and I was finding them to be the only time my mind shut up. You might think sleeping would be good, but I kept dreaming about that blond-haired alien with the hole in his chest.

One foot in front of the other, one breath at a time.

HE HAD SHOCKINGLY RED AND WHITE SKIN STREWN WITH freckles. Nestled in his oval face were playful green eyes and he was wearing a big smile when I saw him.

I was on mile twelve of my run, my body worn and past the point where it longed to stop and rest. I rounded a corner and there he was sitting on a rock. The trailhead, and my car, were about a mile farther. It was late afternoon on a Wednesday and I hadn't seen anyone on the trail at all.

He was dressed to run, but he didn't look like much of a runner. Too short, too happy. As I rounded a corner, he waved at me. I gave him a brief nod and kept running. I knew who he was, but I wasn't going to say anything.

I heard his feet behind me, the rhythm of his feet faster than mine because of his shorter stature.

"Hey, fella," he began. "How's it goin'?" His voice was high with the distinct lilt of an Irish accent.

I was too far into the run to want to talk. I was at that point when the world closed in around me, and all I could see was the trail in front of me. I didn't want to talk. I didn't want to interact. I just wanted to keep running.

"Fine," I answered.

"Nice form there, friend. Ya been runnin' long?" He spoke in short, rushed sentences, the words exploding from his mouth.

I ignored him. I thought about increasing my pace, but I didn't really have enough energy left for that. I took a drink from the tube that led to the water bladder in the little pack on my back. Dehydration was something I had to avoid. I needed to be ready to change to Neutrinoman at any moment, and starting out dehydrated wasn't smart.

"You know," he continued, "I heard ya were a rather decent fella. Kind to strangers. Ready to rescue cats out of trees for little old ladies at the drop of a hat. A real Boy Scout. But I guess not. Too busy running to talk to one of your own."

I was mad. This was *my* time. This was what I needed to do for me. Now, I understand why he approached me here, it was one of the only times I wasn't surrounded by military. And I had been expecting this. Williams had briefed me to expect a recruitment pitch. But still I was angry and I really didn't have a problem letting it show.

"What do you want?" I asked as I kept my pace up.

"Ya know. Just a few minutes of your time, Mr. Nichols."

"What for, Mr. Lucky?" I said. I knew he didn't like being called that.

"Hey!" he yelled. I got why he didn't like that name— after seeing him with his red hair perched on the boulder it was obvious. Dress him in a little green suit and shiny black shoes and you'd have yourself a leprechaun. Not that I thought the name Chaosboy was any more dignified.

I looked down and saw that one of my shoes was untied. I grumbled and came to a slow stop, putting my foot on a rock and slowly tying it.

"Lucky break, that," Chaosboy said as he stopped next to me, his breath coming in ragged gasps. He really wasn't a runner.

"You did this?" I asked as I finished tying it.

He shrugged. "I just need a few minutes."

I started walking and took a big drink. I had to cool my body off. After a run that long it wouldn't do to just stop. "So start talking," I said with a sigh. My legs were jelly and it did feel good to be just walking. I was wearing shorts and the little backpack, no shirt, letting my body soak up as much sun as possible. I was in the reactor every day or so at this point, but I always loved the little boost the Arizona sun gave me. My skin was pale, despite all the sun. Radiation and me, we have a unique relationship.

"Toxic, he wants to talk to ya," Chaosboy began. "He's impressed by ya. He thinks you would be just the addition we need at LoVE."

"Love?" I asked.

"Yeah. League of Villains, Extraordinaire. L-O-V-E."

I groaned in response.

"It was you're idea, ya know. Toxic said ya gave him the idea when you asked him if we were 'a league of villains, or something.'"

I groaned again.

"Come on. It's a great name. Ya know, who can argue against love?"

"I'm sorry, what was the point? I got lost in all that blabbering." I felt bad when I said it. Actually, I felt more embarrassed than anything. It was the kind of thing Toxicwasteman would say.

I heard him stop, so I stopped, turned, and faced him. His arms were crossed and he was looking me up and down.

"What?" I asked.

"Toxic, he was right. He said the Battle at Yellowstone and losing your girl would change ya. He said there was a good chance ya would come in. I didn't believe him. But I kinda do now."

I shrugged, turned my back on him, and kept walking. The grumpy tact was proving effective so I decided to keep it up. Besides, I had a lot to be grumpy about.

"So ya gonna come in? Ya gonna hear what he has to say?"

"Why should I?" I kept walking and he trotted up and was now walking besides me.

"Survival, lad. The military has its head so far up their own arses they can't even breathe. Gotta be nimble with this. Military is anything but. We want the same thing. We want those alien bastards dead and gone. Our goals are your goals."

Chapter 2

Recruitment

Late Winter 2005, Superstition Mountains, Arizona

WE WALKED DOWN THE TRAIL IN SILENCE FOR A BIT, PAST tall saguaro cactus, mesquite trees, and stunted sagebrush. It was the kind of location you might film some miners and their donkeys heading out for gold in the 1800s. The sun was warm and I was enjoying the quiet.

"It's Chaos, ya know," the redheaded youth said, breaking the silence.

"What?" I asked, stopping and looking at him.

"I am not a boy. I turned twenty-one this year. It's 'Chaos.'"

I rolled my eyes and shrugged. I wasn't at all interested in what he wanted to be called. "What is it that you wanted? Aren't we a little off track here?"

"This war with the Arcturian Alliance. It's no conventional war. The stakes are mighty high. The military can't innovate quickly enough. Hell, they need a written order just to take a shite. What this world needs is a small agile group of powerful, dedicated individuals."

"That may be true, but you guys are a league of villains.

I am not a villain. I am not an ends justifies the means kind of guy."

"So, theoretically speaking, what would ya do if ya were confronted with a choice? The stakes are the entire world. You can save it, but one innocent person will die."

"This is ridiculous," I said. "It's never like that. It is never that clear-cut."

"Say it was."

I shrugged. "Well, yeah. I would do it."

"Okay, now say it is a thousand people. No, make it a million. Would ya do it knowing a million people would die?"

"No, of course not. I would find another way."

"There is no other way. Ya can save the world, but a million people die."

"This is ridiculous," I said and started walking away.

Chaosboy ran ahead of me and got in my way. "It's not. One million out of six billion—that's like one tenth of one percent. That kind of loss is not acceptable to ya?"

"No."

"We are talking about saving everyone on the planet."

"I'd find another way."

"Ya really are a Boy Scout. No, I take that back. You're a do-gooder nun. No, that's not good enough. You're Mother freaking Teresa."

"Then I see no reason to come talk to Toxicwasteman."

"It's Toxic, now. We're all going by shorter names. Like, you'd be Neutrino. Nice ring to it, eh?"

I picked him up and put him down on the side of the trail and continued walking.

"I'll make it worth your while," he said from behind me. I could hear him scrambling to catch up. I just kept walking. "I have some information that ya need. I guarantee ya it will be worth it."

He was really starting to annoy me. "What is it?"

"I need your word first."

"Oh..." I began as I stopped and faced him. "Now you want this Boy Scout's word. Now you care about integrity? When it means you'll get what you want it counts."

He nodded and smiled.

"You have my word that if the information you have is valuable to me I will come and talk to Toxicwasteman."

"And... and ya won't reveal the location of our secret base." He seemed to be warming up to this.

I just stood there with my arms crossed.

He waved his hands in a placating gesture. "Okay. Okay. Ya gave your word, that's good. That's good. I only need one more thing."

HE WANTED PROOF. THE LITTLE GUY WANTED PROOF THAT I was Neutrinoman. It seemed ridiculous to me—he had spent the last twenty minutes pestering me.

I had changed my finger for him until it glowed yellow, but that hadn't been enough. He wanted a full body change. I grumbled but in the end I agreed to do it.

I took us off the trail a bit until I found a large boulder that would afford me some privacy. I had a suspicion that he had other motives for this.

"Satisfied?" I asked him as I stepped around the boulder fully in my neutrino form.

He nodded. "That is impressive."

"So tell me the truth now, why did you have me do this. You knew who I was."

He looked a little sheepish. "Our simulations showed there was an 80 to 90 percent chance ya had a subcutaneous tracking device."

I shook my head. "Why didn't you just ask me?"

He shrugged.

I went back behind the rock still shaking my head. Not out of annoyance at his antics, but because he had been right. I did have a tracking device—at least until I had changed—the military had been expecting this offer.

SEEING CHAOSBOY BEHIND THE WHEEL OF THE HUMMER H2 was kind of funny. He really was short, maybe five foot, and the vehicle just overwhelmed him. We had just left the parking area, headed towards Phoenix.

"So," I began. "What's this valuable information?"

He turned and smiled at me. "You're gonna love this." He then told me my full name, the full name of both my parents, the names of Licia and her parents, and the address where we all lived.

"Stop the car," I said, my teeth clenched.

"No. No. Don't freak out, now. We've known for over a month. Took our girl, Byte, all of ten minutes to get the info."

"Stop the damn car."

"We haven't used that information," he said, glancing at me. "We won't. We were just looking into your background."

"What are the odds that you could survive if I exploded right now?" I asked. "Can you bend probability that much? Stop the car."

He pulled the car over and followed me out. We were still on a little two-lane road in the middle of nowhere. I felt a little dizzy. I walked out into the desert with just enough awareness to step around a big bunch of prickly pear cactus.

"Sorry, fella," he said as he ran out to catch up with me. "I said that wrong."

"You think? You better tell me something, right now, or I'll—"

"The media, they've been digging too. Diane Madison, that reporter from WNN, she's got a team on it. They're gonna find out who ya are, who your family is any day now. Ya need to call them."

I sat down on the sandy ground and got my sat phone out—the military had finally issued me my own satellite phone (aka batphone).

"Told ya it would be worth it," Choasboy said with a grin.

I SAT ALONE IN THE DESERT. I HAD YELLED AT CHAOSBOY until he went back to the Hummer. He seemed hurt, like a puppy who had just done a trick and was anticipating a reward, but got scolded instead. The phone I dialed just kept ringing and ringing. It wouldn't go to voice mail, it was another batphone.

"Hello," she said, finally. My heart thudded in my chest on just hearing that one word.

"Hi, it's Nik."

"Oh. Hi," Licia said.

It was as awkward as I had feared, but there was nothing to be done about it.

"Listen, I need to tell you something. Something important. I..." I trailed off. I missed her and I wanted to do anything but tell her what I needed to tell her.

"What is it, Nik?"

"Where are you? You're not driving or anything?"

"No. I'm on a break from training. You know, they are crazy about this now."

"Yeah, I know. Look, Licia, I am sorry to be the bearer of bad tidings, but I have it on good authority that some reporter is about to find out who we really are."

"Oh..."

"Who we are, where we live, what our parents' names are."

"I... Oh God, this is not good." Her voice was shaking a bit, which made my stomach feel like it was going to fall out.

"No, not good. Everything is going to change. Again." I wanted to hold her and talk to her. She's probably the only other person in the world that could understand what I was feeling right then. It was one thing to be doing the superhero q-morph thing with the shield of anonymity. It was going to be a completely different thing to be doing it under the glare of public scrutiny. Sitting there I was scared, and I really had no idea how bad it was going to get.

"I... I better go. I better tell my parents, get my stuff out of my apartment."

"Yeah," I said. "Me too."

There was dead air between us. I wanted to say more, I wanted to plead for a chance to see her, but now was not the time.

"Thanks for telling me, Nik."

"Yeah, of course."

The phone went dead.

I SPENT THE NEXT TEN MINUTES ON THE PHONE. I TALKED to my dad and to Colonel Williams. I didn't talk about

Chaosboy or me having agreed to meet with Toxicwasteman. I am sure Williams could guess.

Maybe it was the specter of being outed as a superhero, maybe something else. But sitting there I was quite paranoid that Chaosboy, or maybe someone else from LoVE, was listening. I didn't want to blow this whole double agent thing before it really got started.

Williams agreed to help. He would coordinate getting my parents someplace where the media couldn't find them. It was going to be a circus.

"Thanks," I said to Chaosboy as I got back to the car.

"Worth it, right?"

I nodded.

"I need ya to melt that down now," he said, pointing at the phone.

I shrugged, held the phone out the open window and let my hand, which was holding it, go moderately neutrino and it became a smoldering pile of plastic and electronics. They didn't want the military to track me. So be it.

He then handed me a black bag and told me I needed to put it over my head.

"Seriously?" I said.

He nodded. "Secret base, ya know. Ya ain't one of us. Precautions, they got to be taken."

I shrugged, putting it on and putting the seat back on the Hummer. I pretended to sleep, but my mind was way too preoccupied for anything approaching rest.

Chapter 3

Chaosboy

Late Winter 2005, Phoenix, Arizona

I HAD TO WONDER ABOUT THE WHOLE BLACK BAG OVER the head thing. Didn't they know who I was? Didn't they know how I became Neutrinoman? My hearing and sense of smell were better than human norm. Even though I couldn't see, I could tell a lot of what was going on.

Not that it was that surprising. We got on the Superstition Highway and headed west; the sounds of the surrounding buildings and traffic confirmed that. We headed north, on the 101. The afternoon sun made the direction obvious. We ended up at a small airport in Scottsdale.

Hell, I really didn't need to have good senses to tell where we were. Just the noise and the sun was enough, and knowing the area.

But, I played along. This was the game, why the hell not?

I was still in a foul mood... and scared. Scared of the life that was coming. Scared that I would never get Licia back, scared of the alien threat of annihilation that hung over it all.

Chaosboy kept up his percussive yammering the whole

way. I couldn't tell if it was to distract me or because he couldn't help himself. Most of it was inane stuff about gambling and sports. But some of it was interesting.

"Toxic is a genius, ya know. That saying, 'the smartest guy in the room.' That's him, all right. It's always him. He's the smartest fella in the room.

"You're gonna love Byte. She's smart and she's... well wait until you see her. She's quite the bird. That'll take your mind off that little ole firefly of yours.

"It's the Greys we need to get. They are from Zeta Reticuli. Mean little bastards. All those stories about alien abductions. That's them. They're the ones. Those stories of anal probes—that ain't bullshit. They get their kicks out of that kind of stuff.

"Ya ever seen a crop circle? Up close? It's freaky. Toxic had me researching them early this year. He's convinced its aliens. Not the Zeta, too creative for them. But some other race. He's thinks they're trying to communicate with us. Maybe trying to help us.

"I heard ya been to Area 51. Did ya get to see the remains of the ship? Damn military has known about all this for sixty years. They just sat on their hands. What a waste. They could'a been ready for them. But it's down to us, Neutrino. It's down to us."

Once we were on the plane, Chaosboy took the black hood off.

"Thanks," I said.

He nodded. We were in a small gulfstream jet. The shades were all drawn on the windows.

He gave me jeans and a T-shirt in my size, so I changed out of my running clothes and we soon took off and headed north. The sun was up, so even with the shades down the direction we were headed was obvious. We were in the air maybe thirty minutes and we landed.

My heart leapt. Flagstaff. Licia might be up here. It was a stupid and childish thought, and I kinda hated myself for having it. But what is that saying? The heart wants what the heart wants. Duh.

The plane braked really hard and fast and the bag went back on over my head. As soon as we got out of the airplane I knew it wasn't Flagstaff. It was cool, but not freezing cold. We must have gone farther north. I suspected the little air-port at the Grand Canyon.

The noise as we drove confirmed my suspicions. We weren't in a city the size of Flag. The drive took a while and was slow. We eventually ended up on a dirt road and things got real slow.

"So, why do you believe in him?" I asked when Chaosboy had finally run out of things to babble on about.

"Toxic?" he asked.

"Yeah. Why?"

"Like I said, he's smart. He knows what he's doin'. He's got a plan. And..." He trailed off and I heard him sniff. "All my life people, they never gave me a chance. Being short I got pushed around a lot in school. Got picked last for sports. Girls weren't very interested. But Toxic, he gave me a chance. He gives me responsibility. He trusts me."

"How did you meet?"

"Do you know my origin story?" he asked.

"I don't," I said, although Toxicwasteman had shared some of it on our way to Yellowstone.

"Well, ya know. It was that day. That day we all changed. I was in Vegas down on Freemont Street. They got this crazy zip line that's, like, seventy feet above the street. The street's all blocked off now, and at night it's full of folks gone in the head. People in costumes. Bands. Things projected on that long-ass awning they have over the street. A lot of fun, really.

"I was really diggin' the zip line and kept doin' it over and over. I was working in Vegas, fixing slot machines. Anyway, Queen was on the awning, singin' 'We Will Rock Ya' while I am sailing above the street. And then the freakiest stuff starts to happen. It's like one of those crazy machines, where the domino falls and triggers the match, which lights the stove, which heats the pot, the steam of which inflates a balloon, which—

"You mean a Rube Goldberg device?" I interjected.

"Yeah, yeah, that. For me it was a Michael Jackson impersonator doin' the moon walk who bumps into the tourist takin' a picture of me, who stumbles in the crowd as he presses the button. His flash blinds this cowboy from Montana who stumbles into a biker from Omaha. The biker takes a swing at the cowboy. Now, some of this I see as I am streaking along. Some of this I put together later. Got lucky and found people who had seen it all.

"Anyway. The cowboy had friends and so did the bikers. A nice, lovely brawl ensues. Security on their goofy Segways head down from just past where the zip line starts. There's this big scaffoldin' and pylons that anchor the thing. The rent-a-cop bumps into a little ole lady who gets her favorite scarf stuck on the little linchpin that anchors the cables to the pylons. She yanks hard and it comes out. Shouldn't matter, right? But there's this lady with a cane in a dirty weddin' dress. She loses her balance and stabs out with her cane and the pin pops out.

"Shouldna happened. The odds, they were a billion to

one. But when the thing was built they had trouble with that pin. The worker put some WD-40 on it to get it in place. That bride popped it right out and down came the zip line I was ridin' on.

"So there I am fallin'. My too short a life flashin' in front of me eyes because of some freak accident that should never have happened. Sixty feet up and hard pavement below. I am gonna die. But I don't. I crash into this booth where people sit around with tubes in their noses sucking on colored oxygen. By some miracle the booth breaks me fall. I walk away unhurt.

"The cosmic rays did their thing. The odds against it happenin' were as high as the odds of me landin' unscathed. I was the luckiest guy in the world. I walked right into the Golden Nugget and started gamblin'. I couldn't lose."

He went silent as we bumped down the road. "You didn't tell me how you met Toxicwasteman," I finally said.

"Oh, that. He heard about the accident and came lookin' for me. I had been hitting Vegas pretty hard, racking up a lot of wins. Too many. The casinos were banning me. Then they tried to run me out of town. It was like high school all over again. I was surrounded in an alley behind the Golden Nugget. Six big guys. The odds were too far out of my favor to get me out of there without some damage. But I did get lucky. Toxic showed up, showed off, and they went a runnin'." He chuckled before continuing. "I remember what he said. He said, 'You and me, we're gonna go far, kid.'"

Chapter 4

The Pitch

Late Winter 2005, LoVE Base, Near the Grand Canyon

THE LAST PART OF THE RIDE WITH CHAOSBOY WAS VERY slow and very rough. We eventually went into a tunnel before parking.

"Okay," he said. "Ya can take that thing off."

I did and there was not much to see. The headlights on the Land Rover were illuminating the form of Tom Tyree. Tall, gaunt, and middle-aged, he was standing about ten yards in front of the vehicle with his arms crossed. We were in a cave about twenty feet in diameter, with a tunnel behind us and a tunnel in front of us where Tom was standing.

I ignored Chaosboy and got out and walked to Tom. "So, I'm here. What is it that you wanted to say?"

He looked me up and down, frowned, and then smiled. "Is it any wonder she's had enough of you? Always jumping right in, never any foreplay."

I smiled and crossed my arms, matching his pose and expression, and just stood there. I was annoyed, but letting him see it wasn't going to help. Actually I was very annoyed. How is it that everyone always seemed to know my business?

"All right then," he said. "I'll give you the tour."

He took me down the tunnel, harshly illuminated by bare bulbs strung along the wall. We came out into a large cave that was about fifty feet in diameter with a relatively flat dirt floor. There were several tunnels exiting this cave in various directions. In the center of the cave was a round table with chairs set around it. Sitting at it was Charles Calvin, aka Dr. Cheese. He had his round-rimmed glasses and lab coat on.

"You know Dr. Cheese," Tom said.

I nodded and gritted my teeth. I disliked the guy immensely. His super power was the production of enzymes. Doesn't sound like much, does it? But think about it. Enzymes are biological substances that cause chemical reactions. So, the magic that turns milk into cheese: enzymes. Almost all chemical reactions in your body involve enzymes.

Dr. Cheese reached up and took my hand, shaking it. His hand was moist and limp—I wanted to wipe it off, but didn't. He smiled but didn't speak.

We've had our run-ins. He once infected several orchards of oranges in Florida. He would walk past the trees touching each one and infecting it with an enzyme. That enzyme infected the tree and transformed the oranges, turning them poisonous. The poison was subtle, though, and wasn't detected until the juice was in the market. The compound in the juice lowered inhibitions, kind of like being very drunk, and resulted in chaos all over the country for a few weeks.

He never did ask for anything. Once I finally caught up with him, he claimed he had been experimenting. Actually, he called it "my little social experiment."

See why I wanted to wipe my hand? God knows what

kind of enzyme he just infected me with and what kind of chemical reaction it could cause in my body.

I hated the guy, I really did. But I kept my mouth shut and followed Tom.

"This is Byte," Tom said as he introduced me to an attractive woman of about thirty. She was dressed simply, in jeans and a black turtleneck, but she moved in a sensuous way that was quite alluring. "That's B.Y.T.E., you know, like computers. Digital something or another." His hand waved vaguely at the racks of computer gear behind her.

Byte smiled and pushed her shoulder-length blond hair behind her right ear. "A pleasure," she said, shaking my hand. Her grip was firm and confident.

"Byte here is the nerve center of our operations," he said. "She handles communications, research, and simulations."

"Simulations?" I asked.

"We do a lot of mathematical modeling," she said, "looking at odds and probabilities. Attempting to predict future patterns based on historical information. Data mining for unseen trends, that kind of thing." She spoke with an English accent that to my untrained ear sounded like she was well educated.

"We model everything," Tom said. "We don't make a move unless we like what we see in the simulations. In fact—"

"You're going to want to see this," Byte said, looking at me and interrupting Tom. She pointed at a large monitor hanging from the ceiling and it turned on. On the screen was Diane Madison, her perfectly coifed hair and plastic smile making me feel uncomfortable in way I couldn't quite explain.

"Join us at seven p.m. central, eight p.m. Pacific for a WNN exclusive report: Neutrinoman Unmasked. We delve into the real life of this real superhero and explode the secrecy surrounding him and other quantum-morphs."

The screen muted as a commercial for Viagra came on. I stood there staring and blinking at the screen while some grey-haired guy talked earnestly about how happy he was now that his penis works better.

I felt a gentle squeeze of my arm and looked at Byte. The look on her face appeared to be compassionate, genuine. It made me wonder what she was doing here. I looked around and saw that Tom had left and was talking to Dr. Cheese. I looked at her face and head closely. I couldn't see any equipment on her. Like a headset so she could hear what was on WNN. Or a remote so she could turn the TV on.

"You're a..." I stammered.

"Q-morph," she said, nodding her head. "I was a geek in a server room when the cosmic rays hit. I was installing some new servers and some bad wiring sent the Internet flowing through me. Not enough electricity to kill me or anything, but it turned my legs to jelly and I woke up a few hours later and could sense the data going through the air."

I nodded in awe. "Were you bit or anything?"

"You're wondering about the third element. Cosmic rays, plus freak accident, plus gene changing catalyst. Like the rat in your case."

I nodded.

"I had gotten a flu vaccination right before the accident. Near as I can figure, that was the third element."

I nodded, still dazed by where I was, who I was with, and what I had just seen on the TV.

"Do you need to sit?" she asked, taking my arm and guiding me to the table.

When Chaosboy had told me that my secret was about

to come out, I had believed him. It was kind of inevitable. Everyone knew I worked at Palo Verde. Everyone knew that Neutrinoman used it as home base. Starting with a list of employees and with a little effort, it was going to be found out.

But, now that it was happening, I felt extremely disoriented. I didn't sign up to be a superhero, and to this point, anonymity had been one of the only things keeping me sane, giving me a shred of a normal life. And now? I had no idea how I would cope with the world knowing who I was.

"How about some cheese?" Dr. Cheese asked, sliding a plate towards me. The smell was intoxicating and a welcome distraction. "I made it myself," he added. I pushed the plate away.

THE PLAN HAD BEEN A SIMPLE ONE. THE MILITARY WAS expecting Toxicwasteman or one of his people to contact me. When they did, I would agree to a meeting, learn all I could, and then alert the military to their location. They would swoop in and take them all into custody.

Sitting there smelling Dr. Cheese's cheese, reeling from the upcoming outing of me as Neutrinoman, I just had to laugh. It was such a simplistic plan. So easy. So logical.

Except Chaosboy had given me a chance to warn my family. I knew I was supposed to be the hero and they were supposed to be the villains, but it was Toxicwasteman that saved the day when we last met in Yellowstone. He had used me as a pawn in his plan, but he had gotten the job done.

But, what if he was using me as a pawn again? What if he had arranged for this little Diane Madison thing, this unmasking of a superhero?

I was so confused. But sitting there with Dr. Cheese watching him nibble on pieces of cheese was not doing me any good.

"What's with the lab coat?" I asked him.

"Huh?" he asked, pushing his round glasses back into position and brushing at his short grey hair. He was a chubby little dude, built like a fireplug.

"You are always wearing a lab coat. What is up with that?"

"Well, I am a doctor, after all," he said with a sniff.

"Yeah. Doctor," Chaosboy said as he sat down and started eating the cheese. "Oh, man. Cheesy, you've out-done yourself."

"You were a podiatrist before the accident," I said. "Why wear a lab coat now? We're in a cave. There's no one else here."

He pulled the white coat tight, monogrammed on the pocket was "Dr. Cheese." He blinked rapidly, his eyes twitching around before meeting mine. "Do you really want to know?"

I nodded. I didn't know if I did, but staying trapped in my head was not a good thing.

"Branding," he said with a nod, before picking up what looked like a piece of Havarti. My mouth was watering. I was more than a little hungry.

"Branding?" I asked.

"Yes, branding. Depending on how all this turns out, there might be some value in my name and image. Endorse-ments, appearances, product sales. The lab coat is my brand. So I wear it, you never know when you might be seen." His hand hovered over the plate of cheese—he seemed to be deciding between a piece of cheddar or another Swiss. "Are you sure you don't want some?" he asked.

I was worried about them poisoning me, but I was hungry, and the cheese did smell fantastic.

"You know," Tom began as he sat down beside me. "You really ought to consider branding yourself. You could be making a mint off of endorsements right now. Neutrinoman energy drinks, Neutrinoman comic books and movies. LoVE has a team of lawyers on retainer. If you were to join us, we could make all of that happen."

My hand darted out, almost against my volition, and snagged a piece of Swiss. It was amazing; fresh and sharp, rich and creamy. I rationalized that if they had wanted to poison me they already had. If Dr. Cheese had wanted to infect me he could have done it when we shook hands. "Wow," I said, surprised when I heard myself speak.

"No one does cheese like Dr. Cheese," Byte said as she sat down on the other side of me. She placed a large tablet computer in the middle of the table on a stand. She smelled of roses with a hint of patchouli. I didn't recall her having that scent on when we met. I found it a bit distracting.

"Let's do this," Tom said. As I sat there eating some of the best cheese I had ever tasted, Tom and the rest of them made their pitch.

THE LIGHTS IN THE CAVE DIMMED, SEEMINGLY OF THEIR own accord, with a single light shining from above on the table. This left the cave outside the circle of light dark and murky. On the tablet appeared the letters L. o. V. E. in 3D slowly rotating.

"This table," Tom began after clearing his throat, "is

round for a reason. Like King Arthur of legend, everyone here has a voice. Everyone here contributes. Everyone here knows the plan. We have no secrets from each other."

Tom got up and slowly walked around the table. There were eight chairs, but only five us sitting there.

He stopped behind Dr. Cheese, his hands resting briefly on the man's thick shoulders. "Doc here is our medic and our chef. His enzymatic superpowers are useful in a variety of situations. He can cause destruction if need be, or get us through a door quietly and quickly. His enzymes can harm or help depending on our needs."

With a smile Tom moved to Chaosboy. "Chaosboy here is our luck. Everything, and I mean everything, goes better with him. He is our eyes and ears in the world, our talent scout, and the first one to join me."

He moved on to Byte, his hands caressing her hair before going to her shoulders. "Byte here is the nerve center of our operation. She can get us through any firewall, can disable any security system, retrieve for us any data, and takes care of managing our finances."

"I," he began, standing behind his own seat, "am the brains of the operation, and sometimes the brawn. I keep us on mission and on task."

He then moved behind my chair and put his hands on my shoulders. "You, Neutrino, you could be our most power-ful weapon. The aliens fear you, fear your power, and with good reason. We need you to save this planet. We, literally, cannot do it without you."

He sat back down. "Our mission is singular and focused: destroy the alien threat; save the planet; have a party." After a dramatic pause he looked me directly in the eyes and asked, "Will you join us, Nik?"

Interview, Part 1

Late Winter 2005, WNN Studios, Los Angeles

Nik's Note: This interview took place shortly after the events described in this book. Diane Madison played a pivotal role in all of this, so I've interspersed portions of this interview to give you a taste of what she was like back then.

SHE WAS BEAUTIFUL—THERE WAS NO DOUBT OF THAT. But it was a beauty born of manipulation. The professional hair and makeup. The expensive, custom-tailored clothing. The perfectly manicured nails, the dazzling white teeth.

Of course she looked that way. She made her living in front of a camera, and if you are in front of a camera everything is manipulated.

She smiled at me and I hated her.

Diane Madison. She was the one who told the world who I was and here I was in a television studio about to be interviewed by her.

"Just relax," she said with a red-lipped smile. "Just be yourself and answer the questions."

I grunted a reply as a short, round woman dabbed makeup on my face and a tall thin man attended to her.

We were on the set of a state-of-the-art news studio in Los Angeles, surrounded by large screens that displayed the rotating WNN logo.

"Give as complete answers as you can," she continued. "You should be talking more than me, a lot more than me. So, no one or two word answers. Let your answers become stories." I must have looked puzzled, because she elaborated. "Pretend the two of us are alone here. We're sitting at a little round table in an Italian restaurant." She sat behind an ornate glass desk, and I sat at one end of that desk. Nothing like an Italian restaurant. "Pretend we are on a first date, and you are trying to impress me."

My eyes widened and I held my hand up, batting at the makeup lady that was still fussing with my face. "Are you insane?" I asked.

Her eyes grew narrow and she said to the makeup artists, "Midge, Al, can you give us a minute?" The tall man and the short woman nodded and walked away. "You were saying?" she said, prompting me.

"This is not a date, and I don't want to be here," I said, letting my anger get the best of me. "You are the one that sat behind this very desk and told the world my identity, Licia's identity. Do you have any idea what that has done, is doing, to my life? To my family? To her life? To her family? Do you think I asked for this? To have these abilities? To have this responsibility? Who the hell do you think you are to do this to us?"

She smiled and nodded. Her face looking completely relaxed and natural, her composure rock solid. I hated her for that calmness. "I apologize," she said smoothly. "You must know it was only a matter of time until your identity was revealed. Best that it was done by me, by a serious news organization, than by some gossip show or tabloid. We got our facts right, we—"

"Is that supposed to make me feel better?" I said, interrupting her. "That I'm better off because you were the one?" I pulled the tissue paper that was still around my collar to shield my powder blue dress shirt from makeup stains. I stood up and said, "I don't think I can do this."

"Please," she said as she stood up and placed her hand on my shoulder. Now I could see fear in that plastic face of hers, now she looked human. "Please, it's okay. I will take good care of you, Nik." Her green eyes were compelling and deep. They sang to me of compassion and understanding. Her hand on my shoulder was warm as she exerted a gentle downward pressure. I found myself back in a sitting position without remembering the act of sitting. Midge was tucking the tissue paper back around my collar and dabbing at my face. The bright lights of the studio were dazzling. Diane was beaming at me, gently nodding her head.

I was such a fool.

Chapter 5

Time for the Truth
Late Winter 2005, LoVE Base, Near the Grand Canyon

I'M NOT SURE WHAT HE WAS EXPECTING. FOR ME TO JUMP up and down and say, "Yes, I will join your psychotic little band of villains."

I didn't know Byte's history, but everyone else at the table was wanted for multiple crimes. Dr. Cheese had done experiments on people with the orange incident and others. He had also destroyed a bridge in St. Louis and tried to extort millions of dollars out of the city. Chaosboy had taken millions from casinos—not that that bothered me much. And, Toxicwasteman had killed on his post-accident rampage.

I'm not sure what he was expecting. I snagged another piece of cheese and looked back at him, chewing.

Dr. Cheese cleared his throat as he pushed his chair back. "I better get started on dinner."

Choasboy excused himself, saying he had to service the helicopter (I hadn't seen one). The lights in the cave came up and Tom, Byte, and I remained at the table.

"I'll need a little more than a dramatic speech," I said.

Tom nodded. "Just as you predicted," he said to Byte. She nodded in return.

"Predicted?" I asked.

Byte nodded again, her blue eyes bright. "Oh yes, we liberated your psych profile from the military and fed it into my software."

I found myself staring at her, my eyes blinking continuously.

"You're here," Tom began, "sitting at our table. It is time for truth. This is how I was able to predict your behavior during our last encounter. How I was able to use you to neutralize the enemy threat."

I was still staring at Byte, blinking. I started shaking my head slowly back and forth.

"We know you value the truth," he continued. "We know the military has you in an atmosphere where you know little. We would change that."

"How?" I asked, looking at him.

Byte gestured to the tablet which showed a picture of an athletic Asian man. "Timothy Tran, code name Tornado. A storm chaser here in the States, he was caught in a class five tornado the day of the cosmic rays. He can now absorb the energy of a storm and release it at will. He was the one that provided the thunderstorm the day you went after the asteroid."

The screen changed to show a tall, handsome man with jet black hair. "Quinn Rask." He was at the Large Hadron Collider facility when the accident happened. He can control his body on a molecular level. The military is planning on introducing him to you soon. They want to see if he can replicate your powers."

I tore my eyes away from the screen and met Tom's.

They were right, knowing the truth was something I valued, something that had been missing with the military. "And the aliens?"

Tom nodded slowly, a small smile on his lips. "The aliens are bent on our destruction, but they are resource constrained."

"What?"

"Think about it, Nik," he said. I wasn't sure how much I liked him using my real name. "If they had the resources to overwhelm us, they would have done it by now. They call themselves the Arcturian Alliance. Arcturus is a star light years away. That they are here is rather astounding. The amount of energy they must have expended to come here was tremendous. They are resource constrained."

I nodded, it was starting to make sense. "But why do they want to destroy us?"

"I don't know. They didn't tell me."

"And what do your simulations tell you?" I asked, looking at Byte.

She smiled, I think she liked the fact that I was catching on. "Not a bloody thing. We don't know them well enough to simulate their psychology. But we have simulated their actions, which confirms that they can't, right now, overwhelm us with force."

"If I had to guess," Tom said, "they thought the asteroid would do the trick. They weren't counting on you, my friend."

I HAVE TO ADMIT I WAS TEMPTED. BACK THEN MY WORK with the military was challenging and often frustrating, but things were good. The lack of information was a constant irritation. They knew more, they just didn't tell me until I "needed to know."

That whole "round table" thing may have been all show, may have been because they knew enough about my psychology and were using it to manipulate me. Maybe. Either way, it was working. I liked the free exchange of ideas. I liked that information was actually flowing to me, that things were actually making a bit more sense.

The three of us talked for another hour or so. I closely watched the interplay between Byte and Tom. She looked at him like... like I wanted Licia to look at me. It wasn't clear to me what stage their relationship was in, but it was clear that there were feelings.

"So," I began after things had quieted down. "So, you have a psychological profile on me. How did you get it?"

Byte shrugged and pushed her blond hair behind her ear again. "Since the accident, firewalls aren't much of an impediment, really none at all."

"And you know a lot about me. About what would tempt me to join you?"

Tom nodded and smiled. This new Tom was kind of freaking me out. He wasn't acting crazy all the time. Sure there were hints of the Toxicwasteman I met at Big Al's Truck Stop, but it was subtler, less obvious. The broad smile, the widening of the eyes at odd times. If I didn't know better, he just seemed like a smart man, if a bit eccentric.

"So everything you are doing," I continued, looking at Tom, "everything you are showing me, even the way you are acting could be to manipulate me. This round table, that timely warning about my identity being outed, you suddenly acting like a sane man. All of it could be put on."

Tom smiled, and the wolfish smile freaked me out and

made me comfortable at the same time. It was the old Toxicwasteman. It was my enemy. But the smile didn't last long and he seemed perfectly sane again. "You could be right," he said with a sigh. He stood up and started pacing around the round table. "We are guided by Byte's simulations. They are not always right, but they are always useful. And, of course we are trying to manipulate you. We want you to join us. That is truth and we only speak truth at this table. But what you see, how we act, that is real. Maybe I appear sane here because I am at home, I am among my people." He stopped directly across from me and leaned on the empty chair. "We need you, Neutrino. We can't defeat the aliens without you. Will you join us?"

I narrowed my eyes and studied him. He seemed earnest. I believed he wanted to end the alien threat, but I worried at what cost.

"Were you, in any way, involved in my identity being revealed?" I gestured to the screen we had seen Diane Madison on earlier.

"No," he said without hesitation. "We've known who you are for months. If we wanted to out you or hurt your family we could have done that. Easily."

I nodded and sighed. I found myself believing him. Hell, I wanted to believe him, that we were fighting the same enemy, in some ways on the same side. I was tired, and I was confused. "I... I need to think about this."

Chapter 6

Eating with the Enemy
Late Winter 2005, LoVE Base, Near the Grand Canyon

DINNER WAS SIMPLE, BUT GOOD. DR. CHEESE SEEMED to have a flair for cooking. The steak was unbelievably tender, the baked potatoes soft and fluffy, the green beans fresh and flavorful.

I ate fast and kept my mouth shut, watching how everyone else acted. We sat around the round table in the middle of the cave.

"How's the planning going?" Tom asked Byte. "Did you get the details you needed?"

She nodded while she chewed. "Everything looks good. Sims look good. But..." her eyes darted to me. "We're going to need everyone to get in and out quickly."

Tom nodded. "It'll be okay."

I let the exchange pass. Clearly there was something else coming down the line. The conversation turned to sports, and some bets were made on the upcoming Eagles/Patriots Super Bowl game.

As I watched I got to know them a bit better. Dr. Cheese was introspective and spoke slowly. Chaosboy continued with his short bursts of words, often ill considered. He was frequently the brunt of jokes. Byte seemed to be all business, except for the way she looked at Tom. And Tom... well, he was like a chameleon. With Dr. Cheese he was careful and intellectual, with Chaosboy he was jocular and funny, with Byte he was focused and intent, and with me... With me he was earnest and serious.

"It's time," Byte said after everyone had finished eating.

The large screen turned on and Diane Madison was speaking. "Neutrinoman, Lightningirl, The Hammer, Toxic-wasteman, Chaosboy, Dr. Cheese." There was some cheering when she mentioned the last few. "Who are these people, who are they really, and what do they mean to us? In the next hour we will explore the origins of these heroes and villains and unmask at least one of them. The WNN investigative team has been working for the last year, and tonight we bring you exclusive coverage as we unmask Neutrinoman."

"Who wants some popcorn?" Dr. Cheese asked. The mood around the table seemed to be cheerful, too cheerful for me. It wasn't their lives that were about to crumble, but mine.

"Excuse me," I mumbled as I got up and left the table. I didn't know where I was going, I only knew I couldn't sit there and watch. I wandered past Byte's equipment and into a tunnel. I had no idea where it led. I really didn't care.

I missed Licia horribly right then. I knew she must be going through something similar. I could almost see us sitting together on a couch, hands clutched tightly as we watched. Not sitting around eating popcorn while a bunch of outlaws cheered.

The tunnel was pretty narrow, the footing uneven—I had to pay attention. As with all the tunnels, it was lit by bare bulbs strung along one side. My mind began to wonder at and focus on my surroundings. Where was I? North of Flagstaff, presumably, but not that far north. There is not much there, a few small towns and lots of desert, and the Grand Canyon. That tickled something in my mind. Tunnels and the Grand Canyon. Maybe this was—

"I'm sorry," I heard an English-accented female voice say. Her voice was a touch husky and I could smell roses and patchouli.

"Thank you," I said without turning around.

"This must be so hard for you." She placed her hand on my shoulder. Her touch was soft and gentle. "No one knows about me, there is nothing to unmask." With her hand on my shoulder she moved until she stood in front of me. Her presence was decidedly feminine—she filled out the turtle-neck nicely—and very distracting. I had all these feelings for Licia that longed for expression but had nowhere to go.

"I..." I stammered.

She laughed, her red lips parting to show perfect white teeth. "Come on," she said, grabbing my hand. "I want to show you something." I let her pull me forward down the tunnel. "It can be such a boys' club in there. I sometimes need to get away. Need to be alone."

A dim part of my mind was screaming that I shouldn't go with her. That this wasn't right. That Licia would not approve. But my need for escape overrode that voice and I went with her. The tunnel curved and we soon came to the end of the lit section and she grabbed a large flashlight and handed me one.

We went into a smaller tunnel that sloped down. Soon I could smell moisture with a slight metallic tinge and could hear dripping.

She laughed and continued to pull me forward. Our light beams suddenly stabbing forward into what seemed to be a vast emptiness and I could hear the sounds of dripping water echoing through the large cavern.

"Where are we?" I asked.

She laughed again, it was soft and gentle, and echoed through the cavern. "Wait till you see," she whispered as her lips brushed my ear. As lights started to slowly come up, I caught my breath. "Oh, my God."

She laughed again.

WE STOOD ON THE EDGE OF A LARGE CAVERN, I COULD hardly breathe. Stalagmites thrusting up from the ground, stalactites hanging from the ceiling dripping water into the pools below. Rocks that sparkled in the artificial light, throwing off sparks of rainbows. Dark water pooled in the center of the cave.

"Come on, Nik," she said, taking my flashlight, setting them both down, and pulling me farther in.

My troubles were forgotten in that moment and I followed her. She treaded a careful path through the cave, sharing its wonders with me: quartz crystals bigger than my leg; smooth limestone formations; geodes bigger than my head. I had seen caves like this before on family outings, but never one where I could linger, where I could explore.

Byte didn't speak much, just now and then pointing out this wonder or that. She eventually led me into a side cavern, and my breath caught again. It was small, maybe ten feet in diameter, and I had to duck to get in the entrance. But it was amazing. The whole cave was a geode, the inside of its surface covered in crystals that went from white to purple. There was a light mounted on the ceiling that made the whole cave sparkle.

"My God," I said.

"This is my place, my little sanctuary," she said, drawing me farther in. We were walking on a narrow wooden path that must have been put there to preserve the crystals underneath.

In the center of the cave was what I would have to call a nest. It was a large pile of blankets and pillows. Byte sat down on them and beckoned to me.

"Um…" I began, looking back and noticing that the lights to the main cavern were off.

She smiled. "Don't worry, Nik. I don't bite. Not at all."

"Cute," I said, but didn't laugh at her little byte/bite joke.

"Oh, come on, be a sport. Relax. Have a seat."

"You know," I said. "I'm a little confused. Aren't you and Tom a couple? Wouldn't he—"

"Yes we are," she said cutting me off. "And no, he's not like that. He's not the jealous kind."

I swallowed hard, I had been guessing at her intentions, and now they were clear. "Yeah. I am kind of involved with someone, not that I don't appreciate the offer."

"I thought she broke up with you."

"Well… Yeah… yeah, she did. But it's not a breakup that I am willing to accept." I was looking out the entrance wondering if I could neutrino-ize my hand and create enough light to find my way out. Did I even know the way out?

"Maybe I can help," she said. "I am a woman. Maybe I can help you understand her motivations."

I looked at her, my eyes narrowing. Something clicked in my brain. "You have her psych profile, don't you?"

She smiled demurely and nodded.

I shook my head. "No, no. That wouldn't be right. That wouldn't be fair."

She laughed. "You really are a Boy Scout, aren't you? Tom said you were. I just wasn't sure I believed him." She sighed and got up, the lights in the cavern slowly coming up. She moved around me to leave the crystal cavern.

"Wait a minute," I said. She turned and looked at me. "You simulate everything, right?" She nodded. "So you simulated this." She nodded again. "And what did your simulation tell you? That I would go for this?" I glanced back at the nest of blankets and pillows.

She smiled, her hand coming to my chest and resting there. "My simulation told me I didn't have a snowball's chance in hell."

"So why?" I asked.

"A girl's got to challenge herself sometimes, doesn't she?" She paused, rising to her tiptoes and kissing me on the cheek. "Besides, I wanted to know if you were really that pure. Not many are, and considering how powerful you are, I think it's a bloody good thing. I think it may help in the end."

Chapter 7

A Gift for Neutrinoman
Late Winter 2005, LoVE Base, Near the Grand Canyon

"Did you show him his quarters yet?" Tom asked with a wicked smile. He had been waiting for us at the entrance to the large cavern.

I think I flushed red. I thought he asked if I had seen Byte's quarters. We had slowly walked our way back up from the cave.

"Nope," she said letting go of my arm and kissing me on the cheek again. "Be nice now, Tom. Our boy's had a tough day."

Tom's grin became even wickeder as he nodded. Byte walked past us and my eyes followed her down the corridor.

"She's quite the woman, isn't she?" Tom asked.

I nodded. "Makes me wonder what the hell she is doing with you."

I expected a retort, but he snorted and said, "I wonder the same thing too."

I just stood there staring at him. I couldn't get a bead on who this new Tom Tyree was and it was keeping me off balance.

"Follow me," he said, taking me down the corridor Byte and I had just come up and then down a new tunnel. He was silent, and that worked for me, so I just followed. We walked for a few minutes until we came to a wide passageway that led to an elevator.

Not the kind you would find in a building, but a rusted metal cage that went down into the Earth. The kind of elevator you would find in a mine.

We got in and went down, I couldn't tell you how far, but it was a ways. At the bottom, the elevator opened up into a warren of tunnels. I began to worry why Tom had brought me down here. I took a deep breath and let it slowly out. It smelled of damp stone, but somehow I liked it down here. I felt at home down here.

I could see that lights were strung along all the tunnels, but only one set was on. Tom handed me a flashlight, keeping one for himself, and said, "Just in case."

We went down the lit tunnel several hundred yards and he stopped. "This is as far as I go," he said.

I was confused. He had said something about my quarters, but why would they be way down here?

He laughed, the sound echoing down the tunnel. "I believe in equitable exchanges," he began. "You came here, which I appreciate, so down that corridor is a gift. A gift that far exceeds the worth of you listening to me. A gift that, I think, you will find very valuable."

I was puzzled as to what he was referring to, but got a glimpse of what was going to come next. "And you are going to want me to even the exchange?" I asked.

He nodded. "In the morning I am going to ask you to do something. You are not going to want to do it, but I ask you to keep an open mind. To look at the big picture." He glanced at his watch and added, "I'll meet you back here at seven a.m."

With that he walked back towards the elevator. When he was gone I took a deep breath and slowly let it out. I really liked it down here. I felt good, peaceful.

I made my way down the tunnel another hundred yards until I came to large metal door. Hanging on it was a white robe, which I ignored for the moment. The door groaned as I opened it and what I saw made me smile.

It wasn't much to see, a small cave filled with a sizable pile of dull grey rocks. In one corner were a cot, a lamp, a little cooler, and a makeshift toilet.

I took a deep breath and took in the ambiance of the place. Those rocks were radioactive. Uranium. I was in a uranium mine, and Tom had set my quarters up in a cave filled with uranium ore. He was right, this was a big gift.

I closed the door, going back out into the tunnel and removed all my clothes and put the robe on. No need to expose them to the radiation.

I went back into my quarters and found the cooler filled with cheese. I smiled, had a piece, and lay down on the cot. Before I knew it, I was asleep.

IT WASN'T QUITE LIKE SPENDING THE NIGHT IN REACTOR number three at Palo Verde, but it was not bad. I had never imagined I would find a charging source that didn't involve the government.

In the morning Tom escorted me back to the elevator, up to the main level, and down another series of tunnels.

"What is that?" I asked as I saw a bright light at the end of the tunnel.

Tom just smiled and beckoned me forth. The tunnel narrowed and ended overlooking a canyon, the morning light illuminating us.

The canyon was deep and beautiful with tan rocks and pinion trees clinging to the sides. I saw several ravens cawing and circling in the bright blue sky.

"The Grand Canyon?" I asked.

Tom nodded. "We are west of the National Park. If you follow that canyon it leads to another canyon which leads to the Colorado River."

"Why?" I asked. "Why are you showing me this?"

"Consider it a gift," he said.

"That you are hopeful I will reciprocate," I said.

He nodded. "I am. I really want you to join us, Nik. But more than that, I want you to have a place, a place not dependent on the military, where you can charge yourself. Where you can carry on the fight with or without the government."

I pursed my lips, worried about what was to come.

"Oh, relax," he said, slapping me on the back. "It's just a fun little heist. No worries."

Interview, Part 2

Late Winter 2005, WNN Studios, Los Angeles

"TONIGHT ON *REAL LIFE WITH DIANE MADISON*," THE announcer's disembodied voice said, "Diane sits down for a live, exclusive, and face-to-face interview with Nik Nichols."

"Just relax," Diane said to me, her voice gentle, her green eyes soft. "It's going to be okay."

I nodded, taking a deep breath and tuning out the announcer. Phrases like "alien threat," "planet killing asteroid," and "global catastrophe" filtered through but I tried to ignore them. I was sweating in the hot lights, and the room smelled of burning dirt, as the lights burned off dirt that had settled on them.

"I think I'm going to puke," I said to her.

"This is important, you know," she said. "What you are doing. The world needs to know."

I nodded but wasn't sure I agreed. The world needed to be saved, whether it needed to know from what seemed to be highly debatable to me.

A droopy-looking man standing next to the camera said,

"In five... four... three..." He mouthed "two" and "one" and pointed to Diane.

"Good evening," Diane began with a smile, looking at the camera. "Just over a year and half ago on September 10, 2003, the world as we knew it changed. It sounds like a bad science fiction movie, but our planet was bathed in cosmic rays and some of us were transformed, gaining unimaginable powers.

"They are called quantum-morphs and of those that have come into the public eye, one stands above the rest as a hero, as—dare I say it—a savior." Her tone was even and believable. I wanted to throw up. "He is called Neutrinoman and it is no exaggeration to say that he has saved Earth and every life on it. To call him a hero is not enough. He is nothing short of a superhero.

"Last month we brought you a special report that revealed this hero's secret identity. Tonight we have the man himself, Nik Nichols, in the studio with us for an exclusive one-on-one live interview. No holds barred, nothing but the truth, real life as it is happening." She swiveled in her chair and faced me. Her red lips were smiling, her wavy black hair glistening under the lights. "Thank you for joining us, Nik."

I licked my lips, swallowed, and nodded my head. I couldn't speak.

"So," she went on. "Just to get this out of the way. You, Nik Nichols, are the q-morph known as Neutrinoman, correct?"

"I..." I began, my voice a croak. "I am, Diane. I am Neutrinoman."

I felt this silence descend around the two of us. It wasn't literal—the studio had been quiet since the show started—it was metaphorical. It was as if the hundreds of millions of viewers had all stopped talking at the same time. As if the attention of the entire world had shifted to me. As if all those millions of eyes and millions of ears were focused on me.

"I am Neutrinoman," I repeated.

Chapter 8

Just a Fun Little Heist

Late Winter 2005, LoVE Base, Near the Grand Canyon

A LARGE FLAT SCREEN ILLUMINATED TOM'S FACE AS HE paced back and forth in front of it. It made his gaunt features look ghoulish, which actually made me a bit more comfortable. Somehow the crazy criminal suited me better than the obliging host. On the screen, Tom was going through a slideshow describing his "fun little heist."

"The diamonds will be guarded with state of the art security," Tom said, pointing to a diagram of a train car that showed positions of guards and the security measures. "You two," he said, pointing at Chaosboy and Byte, "will disable security, Dr. Cheese will take care of the guards, and Neutrino will crack the safe and get the diamonds. I will fly the helicopter and meet you all here." The flat screen showed a desolate stretch of desert between Flagstaff and Winslow. "Any questions?"

No one spoke. I just sat there with my arms crossed slowly shaking my head.

"What is it, Neutrino?" Tom asked.

"I'm not doing it," I said.

Tom stared at me, the fervor on his face when he described the heist fading back into the calm face of the Tom I had known since I got here. "Boys," he said nodding to Chaosboy and Dr. Cheese, "can you please excuse us."

They got up and left, Byte stayed. She was staring at me too. They both kind of had the same looks on their faces, this longing that bordered on lust. They wanted me. They needed me. I wasn't sure why, but I sure as hell didn't like it.

Tom pulled out a chair and sat directly across from me at their round table. "What's the problem?" he asked.

"Oh, I don't know," I began. "First of all, how about this being against the law." Tom's lip curled and his eyes rolled. "And how about how the collateral damage you all are so comfortable with around here. How many people will be injured or killed doing this?"

"Hopefully none," Byte said. "But you are right. We are breaking the law, and some people might get hurt despite our planning. But, the idea is that no one gets hurt, and some big, rich corporation is out a few million in diamonds."

"I won't do it," I said, repeating myself. Tom looked puzzled, which surprised me. "Surely your simulation told you that I would react this way."

Tom nodded. "I was hoping it wouldn't come to this. That we wouldn't have to resort to..." he trailed off.

I hate to admit it, but it got my attention. His big dramatic pause. "What?" I asked.

"There is one more thing we can offer you," Byte said, her face compassionate.

"What?" I asked, louder this time. This drama crap was starting to drive me a little nuts.

"We can tell you how to get her back," Tom said.

"Even though it means you won't be joining us," Byte

added. "Because, let's face it. If she was in the picture, you wouldn't be here right now."

I hate to say it, but I am sure my face showed everything that was going through my head right then. A bit of surprise, followed by the memory of Licia's lips, and then the pain of her being done with me. "How?" I asked, the urgency in my voice unmistakable. It seemed like someone else was speaking. "How do I get her back?"

"First the diamonds," Tom said. "Then we'll tell you."

"No casualties," I said in way of agreement.

Byte nodded. "Let me go over the details with you. There shouldn't be any."

THE PLAN WAS PRETTY SIMPLE. WE WOULD BOARD THE train in Flagstaff, grab the diamonds, and jump the train before Winslow where Tom would pick us up in the helicopter. Dr. Cheese was preparing an "enzymatic concoction" that would render the physical guards unconscious, while Byte would disable the rest of the electronic security. Once in, I would get us through the vault. Chaosboy was there to make sure everything flowed smoothly.

She showed me the simulations she had created and the probabilities of success. It seemed so simple. And the prize on the other side was a way back to Licia.

It was just Byte and me standing in the main cave surrounded by all her computers and monitors. She was looking at me expectantly. I knew she wanted me to tell her that I would do it. That they had followed all the right steps laid out by their simulations and I was now on board. It was strange. I was starting to recognize that expectant look.

"Why are you with him?" I asked instead.

She looked surprised briefly, but then got this faraway look and smiled.

"Tom is..." she began. "Well, Tom is, if nothing else, a huge supporter of q-morph rights. He found me. He helped me before I really understood what was happening to me."

"Found you?" I asked.

She looked at me briefly and then looked away. "When it happened, I was not okay. I was a programmer at Google working at their Kirkland, Washington, campus. I was a search algorithm specialist, programming the guts of their search engine. I loved it. And then the accident happened.

"I was back in the server room gallivanting." She looked away. "Actually, at Google, the server rooms are more like warehouses. It's not hard to find a bit of privacy. My boyfriend at the time was a hardware engineer." Her cheeks flushed red and she looked down. "I don't know, it was exciting. I liked being close to all that data and I liked him.

"It was that day of the cosmic rays. Things got a little out of control, and I ended up naked with my back pressed against some open wiring. It was a rather complicated and expensive router that had much of Google's Internet traffic going through it. The cover was off—it was in the process of being repaired.

"So I had all this electricity going through my skin. Not high voltage, but lots of it. And it wasn't just current, it was information. Too much information. Somehow, because of those cosmic rays, it was almost as if I had ten thousand conversations going through my head at once.

"Well, I was off my trolley then. I ran out of there naked and babbling and ended up getting locked away."

I looked at her. She was lost in her memory, staring at her hands. "And Tom?" I asked.

"He found me. He knew what had happened. He helped me through it."

I nodded. "So, loyalty. That's it then."

"He saved my life," she said. "And now he is trying to save the planet."

I was really having trouble reconciling the Tom I had encountered here, and the Toxicwasteman that had run amok before Lightningirl had taken him down. The Tom that so gleefully manipulated me in our encounter with the aliens.

"I don't trust him," I said. "I don't trust his motives. I don't like how he gets things done."

Byte took a deep breath and let it out in a long sigh. "I get that, I really do. But I think we may have a better shot than the military at defeating these aliens."

"Really?" I asked. "Don't they have a trillion-dollar budget? Don't they have the best weapons and technologies? Not to mention quite a few q-morphs on their side."

"Afghanistan," she said. "Iraq. We've been over there for two years now, with no end in sight. Missing money. Bureaucratic boondoggles. That's whose hands you want to put the fate of the world in?"

"And you want me to trust Toxicwasteman?" I asked. "An unstable psychopath. Someone who would be happy to win, if winning meant half the planet dying. The man that revels in being a villain. The guy that will do and say anything to get what he wants. That guy? Really?" My voice had gotten loud. The rest of the conversations in the cave had gone silent as they listened to me rant.

I felt Byte's hand on mine and smelled her rose scent. "Just do this job, Nik. Please. We can help you get your Licia back."

And that was the thing, right? For what ends would I accept the means? If the prize was Licia, would I be willing to be a thief instead of a Boy Scout? For the woman I loved would I compromise my morals? Actually, this was just their promise that they knew how. So the question was: what would I do for just a chance?

I stared at her and she met my gaze unblinking. "How good is this information?" I asked.

"My simulations give you a 98 percent chance of getting her back with this information. A 28 percent chance without."

"What is your margin of error?" I asked.

Her eyebrow raised, I didn't think she was expecting that. My latest pre-superhero job was as a janitor, but I wasn't a dummy. I had a business degree. And when I had that thought, I had to wonder. Didn't she know that? Was she expecting the question? Was the eyebrow raise part of what her simulations told her to do? The whole "we simulate everything" was starting to drive me absolutely batty.

"Plus or minus 10 percent," she said.

"I don't want to know her deepest darkest secrets," I said. "I don't want to know about her psych profile. I don't want to know those kinds of things until she is ready to tell me."

She smiled. "She's a lucky girl, you know. But, you don't have anything to worry about. What we have is a general strategy. One that is very you, and you might stumble on it yourself. But if you use it, your odds go way up."

The look on her face was one of victory. She had hooked me and reeled me in, and she knew it.

Chapter 9

Collateral Damage
Late Winter 2005, East of Flagstaff, Arizona

As THE HEIST WENT DOWN, IT HAD EVERY APPEARANCE OF being easy. Too easy, really. It was the Chaosboy effect. He had this distant, check-out look on his youthful face most of the time. He was bending probabilities to our advantage. We boarded the Amtrak train at the red-bricked train station in Flagstaff.

I don't know if you've been to Flagstaff, but it's a beautiful little city. The downtown area, where the train station is, caters to tourists and is full of historic brick buildings. Flagstaff itself is at a seven-thousand-foot elevation, but it is dwarfed by the nearby San Francisco Peaks rising behind the city to the north. At 12,600 feet, the mountain is the tallest point in Arizona. Flagstaff is dry, but not what you think of when you think desert. With the mountain and all the towering ponderosa pine trees, it doesn't look like a desert at all.

It was cold, and there were the remnants of the last snowstorm on the ground. We entered the train quickly and made our way to our seats. We were all silent. I sat there thinking of Licia. This was her home. I watched out the window at people driving by on Route 66 or walking in their hats and heavy coats and looked for her. It was silly, I know. I should have been focusing on what I was doing. I should have been keeping an eye on my companions. But I didn't. I just sat there hoping to catch a glimpse of a girl.

Byte was in charge. No one ever said it to me, but it was clear to everyone. Once we had cleared Flagstaff and started making our way towards Winslow, Byte got up and we all followed her. Outside the train, the pine trees had been replaced with scraggly pinon trees as we went down in elevation.

We made our slow way through the passenger cars to the back of the train, the click-clack of the train on the tracks beating out a rhythm. The end of the train held a dining car, a bar car, and then the final car, which was our destination. It was an armored train car. Kind of like those Wells Fargo armored trucks you see picking up bags of money from banks.

We went to the bar. Byte ordered us all lite beers, and we waited. I refused to talk to Dr. Cheese (still dressed in his lab coat, by the way), and Byte and Chaosboy both had these spacy looks on their faces. She was hacking into the electronic security; he was making sure things went our way.

Dr. Cheese downed his beer and then asked for another and then another. This was part of the plan. He wasn't in danger of getting drunk—his body could metabolize the beer in such a way that he didn't get inebriated. Part of that enzymatic superpower thing. He just made sure his stomach was full of enzymes that neutralized the alcohol.

There were about three other patrons in the car and

the bartender. He was an affable-looking young man, with a clean white shirt and short black hair. He gave me a strange look when we came in, but I didn't think anything of it. I considered slipping him a note, telling him to get the patrons out of here. But that wouldn't have helped. I worried about what would happen when we went into the armored train car.

After about thirty minutes, Byte nodded to Dr. Cheese. He stumbled back through the car, looking like a bad actor pretending to be drunk. Byte gave me a pointed look, so I played my part.

I shook my head in disgust and said, "I'll go get him."

When I caught up with him he was in that narrow area between cars, his hand covering the little glass window of the door to the armored car.

I peered in and saw three big guards on the ground, a white mist in the air. He had dissolved a hole in the glass and pushed through his little knock-out bomb.

"Did they see you?" I asked.

"No," he chuckled. "They were all too focused on their card game. That little redheaded kid can really make the impossible happen."

"How long?" I asked.

"The gas will neutralize in another thirty seconds," he said.

I watched as the gas floated to the ground and then disappeared. He got this intense look on his face as he pushed on the glass. Soon there was a hole in the glass in the shape of his hand. He reached through and unlocked the door.

We moved into the car. It was utilitarian with a few seats, steel cabinets, and a big safe. This was what I was here for. Dr. Cheese could get through metal, but not quickly.

I went to the safe and noticed one of the guards. He was twitching with white foam coming out of his mouth. "Shit," I said as I leaned down. I looked up at Dr. Cheese. "What's wrong with him?"

He leaned down, checked his pulse, and pulled his eyelids back. "He's having a bad reaction to my formula."

"I thought you said it was safe?"

"It is. Only one in a million would have this kind of reaction," he said.

I looked at the guard and back to Dr. Cheese. "So what do we do?"

He shrugged, looking at the safe. "We do our jobs."

This was it. This moment. In that train car with Dr. Cheese. My reaction compared to Dr. Cheese's is what made us different. I won't say that mine made me a hero, and his made him a villain—I don't have that big of an ego. But that look of dismissal on his face, how easily he was willing to discard a human life, it did something to me.

I pulled him down by his lab coat and said, "What's it going to take to save him?"

His eyes were wide. I think he was expecting me to act just like him. He looked down at the twitching guard again and said, "He's in anaphylactic shock. He needs a shot of epinephrine. That might do it."

I grabbed under the guard's armpits and started dragging him out of the car. As I pulled him something occurred to me. Why Chaosboy is called Chaosboy. Our ease at getting into the train car with the guards was a million to one in our favor. The odds of this guard getting sick from the gas was a million to one too.

So while Choasboy was creating things favorable to us, he was trailing a wake of bad luck for others. It made sense.

The order of things have to stay in balance. While he creates positive outcomes for us, that has to be balanced by negative outcomes for others.

I squatted down and put the guard over my shoulder. He was bald and about two hundred pounds. I grunted as I stood and started forward.

"Where are you going?" Dr. Cheese asked. "We need to open this vault."

I didn't answer him. There were shouts when I entered the bar car. "He's having an allergic reaction. Does anyone have an EpiPen?"

No one answered. Byte looked shocked and Chaosboy came out of his trance, a look of surprise on his face.

"You did this," I growled at the redhead. "You are going to fix it."

"What?" he asked.

I set the guard down and grabbed Chaosboy by the shirt. "Use your power. We need to find someone with an EpiPen. We need to inject this guy now. He needs to survive. Got it?"

He slowly nodded. I let go of him and watched as his face went blank. I looked at the bartender and said, "Go, find us someone with an EpiPen. There must be someone with allergies that carries one on this train."

He nodded and ran off.

"We don't have time for this," Byte whispered to me. I smiled at her and turned my attention to the guard. His twitching had increased. His skin was blotching and his face was clearly swelling. His breath was becoming labored. I squatted down and checked his pulse which was weak.

I considered going after the bartender, but didn't. I worried that my companions would abandon him. Time was passing with agonizing slowness. I felt helpless. I resolved to get some first aid training so I would at least have a clue what to do.

I looked around, Dr. Cheese had stayed in the other car, and everyone else in the bar car was avoiding me and the guard.

I was about to go looking for an EpiPen myself when the bartender rushed back. "Here," he said, handing it to me. "I found someone with one, only two cars up."

I stared at the directions—I had never done anything like this. It was, fortunately, very simple. I opened the tube, pulled out the injector, and jammed it into the guard's leg, the needle going through the pants as I held it there.

"I'm a doctor," I heard a woman say. I looked up and saw a middle-aged woman, carrying a small bag. "What happened?"

"I found him this way," I said. "He's having some sort of allergic reaction."

She looked from me to the EpiPen that I was still holding to his leg. "It's okay," she said gently. "You did the right thing." She took the EpiPen and leaned down, putting her ear to his chest. "I think he's going to be okay."

I nodded, feeling dazed. Yeah, I know, I have taken on aliens and earth-killing meteors. But this was up close and personal. This was so far out of my depth. I looked around and saw that Byte and Chaosboy were gone.

"Can you..." I began. "Can you handle this? I've got to do a thing."

She nodded, smiling, but the smile soon left her face as her mouth opened. "You're... Aren't you..." she began.

My heart leapt. I had been so caught up in what I was doing that I forgot that my identity had been revealed last night.

"Yeah," the bartender said. "I knew you looked familiar. You're that Neutrinoman, aren't you?" He was speaking rather loudly, and the few other patrons in the car heard and started talking among themselves.

I mumbled something and I felt my face flush red. I surged to my feet and walked back to the armored train car. Time to finish this damn robbery.

Chapter 10

An Unexpected Visitor
Late Winter 2005, East of Flagstaff, Arizona

"OUT OF MY WAY," I GROWLED. DR. CHEESE WAS CON-centrating, his hand against the safe's metal hinges. Chaosboy had his zoned–out look and Byte was looking on, her arms crossed.

I slapped Choasboy on the head. "Stop that. Don't make us lucky unless we really need it. I don't want you putting someone else's life on the line." He blinked and slowly nodded.

I pulled my right sleeve back and turned my right hand and forearm neutrino and pressed it against the hinge. I was full of adrenaline and emotion, from both the guard's medical emergency and being recognized. I was embarrassed, scared, and angry. I took all that energy and funneled it into what I was doing. The metal slowly melted under the pressure of my neutrino hand.

No one spoke to me, for which I was grateful. It was clear from their body language that I was not one of them now. And that suited me fine. The sooner I could be done with this, the better.

The safe was not that complex. I had seen plans of it back in the LoVE hideout. All I needed to do was cut through the two hinges, and the bolt, and the door would open.

It took about five minutes, and worked well enough. Soon the door was open. Byte swooped in and took a small black bag out of the safe, and we were done.

How do you jump from a moving train and land without any major injuries? Well, you are either in an action movie, or Chaosboy is doing his thing. We went out the back end of the armored train car, and they jumped. First Dr. Cheese, and then Byte, and then Chaosboy. One by one I saw them execute graceful leaps and roles as if they were trained stunt men. I saw them stand up and brush themselves off.

I paused. I knew I needed to go. The robbery would be discovered soon and I would probably be implicated. I took a moment and looked out over the brown grasses of the high desert. It was desolate land but beautiful. I heard the approaching thump-thump of a helicopter, I smelled the exhaust of the train, I heard the whoosh of a...

I looked around trying to locate the whooshing noise and spotted a round silvery surface.

Time seemed to slow down. I could hear my heart beating, feel my breath move in and out of my chest. It was an alien ship, much smaller than the one I saw in Wyoming. It was about as big as a helicopter and had that classic "flying saucer" shape.

I smelled smoke and realized that my clothing was burning as my body changed to its neutrino form. Gone was the sound of my heart beating and the in and out of my breathing. I felt a rage deep in me. Forgotten was my revulsion at the death I had caused at Yellowstone.

The three other q-morphs were pointing at the flying craft and then running. The helicopter Tom Tyree was flying came into view. It was one of the helicopters used to fly tourists over the Grand Canyon and had the colorful logo of the tour company emblazoned on it. The saucer oriented itself towards the helicopter and the front section of it began to glow. It was past the train now and I was behind it.

My transformation complete, I found myself flying towards the craft, letting my neutrino reaction burn hot. Things still seemed to move so slowly. The spinning rotors of the helicopter were visible, the fleeing q-morph's movements were comically slow, and my progress was an agonizing creep.

A bolt of white energy leapt from the front of the saucer and stabbed out at the helicopter. Tom must have anticipated the move. The helicopter jogged to the right and the bolt only scraped some of the paint off the side.

I accelerated as hard as I could and right as I came up on the craft it moved suddenly down. Even in this strange slowed-down experience, the move was fast, but not quite fast enough. I adjusted my trajectory as best I could and felt my neutrino form impact the top of the craft. The impact was jarring and painful. I increased my neutrino output in reaction, glowing even brighter.

Time sped back up and I found myself tumbling and falling, glimpsing the burning silver craft as I fell. I impacted the ground and got to my feet as soon as I could. The saucer was twenty yards away, twisted and smoking. I started moving towards it when it exploded, the shock wave knocking me off of my feet.

Interview, Part 3

Late Winter 2005, WNN Studios, Los Angeles

"EARLIER TODAY," DIANE MADISON SAID TO THE CAMERA, "Nik was kind enough to take us for a tour of his home base, the Palo Verde Nuclear Generating Station. It is here that his act of selfless courage saved Palo Verde from a nuclear meltdown, it is here that he first became Neutrinoman, and it is here that he absorbs the radiation he needs to become Neutrinoman." She paused with a big smile on her face that she held for so long, it made me very uncomfortable.

"And we're clear," a voice said out in the darkness of the studio.

The footage they were playing showed me giving a tour of Palo Verde. Showing the coolant valve I had released to prevent the meltdown. I wore a suit and looked quite uncomfortable in it. The monitor on the desk played the video with no audio. It was strange to watch myself like that. The cameraman that was in the reactor with me had on a yellow radiation suit, complete with gloves, mask, and respirator, and I was running around in a business suit. I pulled up my leg and pointed to the place the neutrino mutated rat had bit me. There is a visible scar there. Even after all my transformations to my neutrino form, that scar doesn't go away.

"You're doing great," Diane said. Al, her makeup guy, was touching up her makeup, while Midge worked on mine.

"Oh... Yeah, thanks," I said, my eyes still on the video.

"Just act natural," she said. "Forget the camera and just talk to me. Like we're two friends chatting over a cup of tea."

It was a nice thought. Just two friends, not millions of people around the world watching me. Not being asked questions by one of my least favorite people. Not to worry if I will get the answers right and stay within the bounds of the information the military spent a week drilling into me. This wasn't a simple interview. This was—

"Oh, I love this part," Midge said. I followed her gaze to the monitor. We had come to the point where I was going to transform. This whole thing had been orchestrated by some big PR firm the military had hired. Like the fact that I had a suit on and product in my brown hair. They had made me practice this until I got it right.

I watched the monitor as the transformation occurred. It started in the middle of my chest, the suit smoking, flames licking the edges of the yellow circle that emerged from beneath it. This was what the PR guys had wanted, for the transformation to start in the middle of my chest and spread from there. It had to take twenty seconds, no more, no less. They wanted people to be able to see it, but not get bored.

And why did it have to start in the middle of the chest, you might ask? Well, if you saw it, you probably already know. It looked an awful lot like Clark Kent ripping open his suit to reveal his Superman costume beneath. They were trying to invoke that image, to imprint that heroic mythology on me.

As I watched it happen on the monitor, as I heard Midge and Al gasp in awe, even though they had seen it before, I wanted to run away. I didn't want to be that hero, and I hated how hard everyone had to work to try to create that illusion.

Because to me, it felt like an illusion. I wasn't a hero, much less a superhero. I just happened to have these powers and was trying my hardest to do right by them. I didn't want to be a spokesman. I didn't want to be the public face of the q-morphs and the war against the aliens. In fact, right then and there, I just wanted to throw up.

The footage was soon over, Midge and Al were gone, and the grip, or whatever he was, gave us the countdown and we were back on the air.

"That..." Diane began, the look of awe on her face appearing to be genuine. "Well... I..." she continued to stammer, looking at me and then at the camera. "Ladies and gentlemen, I need a moment, let's take a commercial break. We'll be back in a flash with Neutrinoman."

After the man yelled "clear," Diane's face became controlled again, the emotion that appeared to be so genuine gone in an instant.

"When we come back," she said, "we will be starting the interview. Are you ready?"

I stared at her. How could she turn moods on and off as easily as I turned into Neutrinoman? Was it all a show? What were her real motives? Seeing her like that just fanned the anger I had. The fear of what was happening had quelled it, but seeing her blatant manipulation of everything, I no longer had compassion for her and all that was left was my anger. "No," I said with a smile.

Her smooth forehead creased briefly in puzzlement, before smoothing back out, a smile playing on her lips. "Come now. You've saved the world. Surely a little interview can't be that bad."

"Wanna bet?" I asked. I kept my face as placid as I could. True, I was messing with her, but seeing how she was messing with the whole world, I felt quite justified.

The smile she gave me was full and wide as she slowly shook her head. "You want to play?" she asked, her right eyebrow arching. "Well, let's play."

"In five... four... three..." the man said as we were going live again.

Chapter 11

Farewell to LoVE
Late Winter 2005, East of Flagstaff, Arizona

"That was well done," Tom said. He was in his biological form about ten yards away. I was still in my neutrino form. I considered dropping it, but decided not to. I didn't trust him, didn't trust that there wasn't another ship close by.

I stood up and looked at the smoldering wreckage. Chaosboy was kicking at a piece of twisted silver metal, Dr. Cheese stood back a safe distance, and Byte came up next to Tom and took his arm.

"What the hell were they doing here?" I asked, looking at the ship.

Tom shrugged and looked to Byte. She got this faraway look before saying, "After the diamonds too, I suspect."

"Diamonds?" I asked. "Why?"

She nodded. "Some of the Nordic-looking ones have infiltrated our society. They've been here for years. They need funding, just like we do." She looked at Tom and added, "What now, love?"

"Get everyone loaded," he said to her. "I need to have

a few words with our friend before we go." It sounded like they didn't want me to go with them and that suited me fine.

She walked off and talked to Chaosboy and then Dr. Cheese before heading towards the helicopter. I was standing about one hundred yards off. Dr. Cheese went with her towards the helicopter but Chaosboy ambled closer, a twisted piece of silver metal in his hand.

He saw me looking at it. "Souvenir," he said by way of explanation. I just nodded, my arms folded. "Ya know," he continued, "we made a great team. It's a shame ya won't join us."

I didn't say anything. I just stood there staring at him. Actually, that's not quite the truth. I stood there staring at him and considered killing him. He was close enough that he would not be able to survive the blast if I chose to explode. He couldn't bend probability that far.

And in truth, I was beginning to consider him the most dangerous member of LoVE. The way he could make the improbable happen and leave chaos in his wake was disturbing. That combined with his "who cares about collateral damage" attitude added up to something terrible. But I didn't do it—it wasn't in me.

"It's been a pleasure, Neutrino," he said with a wave of the piece of metal as he turned and headed towards the helicopter.

"It's Neutrinoman," I shouted after him. He turned and gave me a grin and a nod before continuing on. I realized something important right then. Something important about names. Most of these villains wanted to go by these short names: Toxic, Byte, Chaos. It had really begun to bug me and I finally realized why. Having "man" on the end of my superhero name reminded me of my humanity, my connection with the rest of the beings on this planet. No one called Superman "Super," or Spider-Man, "Spider," or Wonder Woman, "Wonder." There was humanity to their names and humanity in their actions.

These villains wanting to discard the "man" or the "boy" seemed symbolic of them wanting to discard their humanity. That they didn't want to be reminded where they came from. In that moment, standing there, it occurred to me that that is what made them villains. And it is why I refused to call them by their abbreviated names. I was hoping to see that humanity in them.

I came out of my reverie to find Tom studying me. His eyes widened and he got one of those crazy grins on his face. Gone was the logical and reasonable Tom Tyree that had been trying to recruit me, and back was the crazy face of the Toxicwasteman that I had first met. "This was fun, wasn't it?" he asked looking around at the wreckage.

"No," I answered.

He nodded. "But you've been a good sport, thanks for playing along. Tell him what he's won, Johnny." His voice changed timber and became like some sleazy radio announcer. "He's won his very own superhero base that he doesn't need to tell the military about. It's stocked with rations and a supply of uranium ore he can use to charge himself in case he ever gets tired of the short leash his military masters have him on."

"I have to tell them something," I said.

"What's that, Johnny?" he said tilting his head and putting his finger to his ear. "There's more?" His voice changed back to the announcer voice. "That's right! There's another abandoned mine close by that he can take the military to. It's an actual former hideout of LoVE complete with tantalizing remnants the military will salivate over." Tom moved closer and showed me his phone. On it were two sets of GPS coordinates, one for the base I had been at, and one for the old base. "Remember these," he said in his normal voice.

"Why are you doing this?" I asked.

"Really?" he began. "Are you that slow? Isn't that obvious by now?" He pointed at the wreckage of the alien craft. "They are afraid of you, with good reason. This world needs you to defeat them. And whether you like it or not, this world needs me and my crew to defeat them too. And you need a source of power not connected to the military. They are going to do something stupid—it's only a matter of time. And when that happens, it can't take you out of the game."

He turned and walked several paces towards the helicopter. "Oh," he said, turning around. "I owe you the secret to your lady-love's heart."

I shook my head. "I don't want to know." I was a bit surprised at the words, but as I thought about it, it made sense. It wasn't me. "I don't want to know what you learned about her in her psych profile. I don't want you to teach me how to manipulate her. I love her and I will never give up. That is enough. That has to be enough."

He slowly shook his head and sighed. "Very well." He again turned to go and then stopped himself. "But, you might want to know of the results of our latest sim. This is in regards to our enemy." He pointed at the wreckage. "We told you they are resource constrained." I nodded. "You also know there are aliens that can pass for us." I nodded again. "We anticipate one more attempt on your life in the near future. One from these embedded aliens."

"Where? When?" I asked.

"We don't know," he answered. "But it will be soon, it will be vicious, and it will be a direct attack on you."

I just shook my head.

"The good news, though," he began cheerfully, "is that after that attack, provided you survive, we expect a long break while they get more resources to our planet."

"Any more good news?" I asked. He smiled and nodded, he seemed to be taking my sarcasm seriously. Maybe he thought this was all good news.

"WNN wants Diane Madison to interview you," he said. "The military brass has decided it's a good idea to do now that your secret is out."

I just stood there shaking my head. It was the last thing I wanted to do. And my anger at being outed was directed at Diane Madison, so she's the last person I would want interviewing me.

"Personally," Tom continued, "I think you ought to do it. If you don't take control of your personal brand, the media will do as they please with it, and that just won't be pretty." He pulled a cell phone out of his pocket and placed it on the ground. "I'd appreciate you giving us a few minutes head start before calling in the troops." He nodded towards the wreckage. "They are going to want to lock the scene down and recover what they can from that."

With that, Tom Tyree turned and trotted to the helicopter. Before he got in, he turned back to me and waved enthusiastically like some six-year-old saying good-bye to Grandma and Grandpa.

Chapter 12

Rescue

Late Winter 2005, East of Flagstaff, Arizona

AFTER THEY LEFT I REVERTED BACK TO MY BIOLOGICAL form and stood there shivering. I grabbed the phone, sent a text to Licia telling her I was about to call and asking her to pick up. I then called her.

"Hi," she said when she answered the phone.

"Hi," I replied back. I was pacing back and forth trying to keep warm. "Umm... I just wanted to see if you were okay after last night's... you know."

"Did you see it?" she asked.

"No. Couldn't watch it. Did they reveal your identity?" I asked.

"Yeah," she said, "and Tom Tyree too. It's all over the Internet, how did you miss it?"

"I've been... away. It's pretty complicated actually. I only have a minute. I wanted to make sure you're okay. Did you get your parents out of town?"

"I did. Thanks for the warning," she said

"Sure," I replied. I cringed, this wasn't going the way I wanted it to. It sounded like I was talking with someone I met once, not someone I wanted to be with.

"I guess I should go too," she said. "More training—we're just on break. Take care of yourself, Nik."

"Wait," I said, increasing my pacing, rubbing my chest with my free arm. "I... I..." I stammered.

"What is it, Nik? Are you okay? Your voice sounds strange."

"Well, I'm freezing, but that's not it. There's something I need to say."

"Umm... Nik, really. I don't think there is anything to say." She sounded a little scared.

"But there is. And I will hate myself if I don't say this. I... I..." I trailed off again like a stammering idiot. There was silence on the other end of the line. I was coming to the conclusion that I didn't really like talking to her on the phone. She was generally all business, and this was definitely not business.

"Nik, I've got to go," she said after a long pause.

"I'm not going to give up," I blurted.

"What?" she asked.

The words, now that they were started, came tumbling out. "I'm not going to give up on you, on us. I will never give up. If there were ever two people in this insane world that were meant to be together it's you and me—"

"Please. Don't," she said.

"I know, I know, you think it makes us vulnerable, you think it makes us weak, you think it interferes with our ability to do what we need to do, to make the hard decisions. But I don't agree. You make me stronger. You give me a reason to fight, a reason to live, a reason to keep going.

"Who else could understand what you are going through today with our identities being revealed, besides me? Who else can truly relate to what we have to go through with these powers, with what we can do, when things go wrong.

"But more than that, I love you, Licia Lopez. More than I thought myself capable, I love you. And you can tell me no today and tomorrow and for every day for the rest of my life, but I will not stop. I will not give up. I will not."

After I was done, there was silence on the line, and then I heard her sniff, she must have been crying. "I have to go, Nik," she said.

"No. Please, don't," I said. "Just talk to me. This has been a bad few days. I—" Movement caught my attention inside the burning saucer. It was a brief flash of something, I couldn't tell what. I moved closer, peering through a large gash in the vessel that ran vertically.

"I can't, Nik. I can't. I'm sorry, I—"

"Holy shit," I said. I had heard her words but they didn't mean much. The gash was ragged metal, and inside the vessel was a flashing light. When it flashed on I thought I could see a humanoid form and hear moaning. "I think he's alive."

"What?" Licia asked. "Who's alive? What are you talking about?"

"Where are you?" I asked.

"Umm... Area 51. Training, I told you that. Why?" she said.

"Okay, good. Listen carefully. I'm between Flagstaff and Winslow next to the train tracks." I said, talking fast, my words punctuated by my chattering teeth. I was naked and the cold was getting to me. "There's a downed alien craft and I think there is a live alien in it. I think he's hurt. There is a fire inside the craft. I am going to try to pull him out.

Tell Colonel Williams. Have him get personnel here as soon as possible."

"Oh my God, Nik. Please, be careful," she said.

"I'm putting the phone down now. Leave the connection open, it might make it easier for them to find me."

Licia was speaking, but I put the phone down anyway. My mind was careening between fear of the alien, fear that I might find another corpse, and excitement at the possibility of talking to a live alien and asking questions.

I stepped away from the phone and changed to my neutrino form. It was a blessed escape from the cold, but that hardly registered. I approached the gash and peered through. There was a small open area in the center of the ship. It was dominated by what looked like a reclined chair. Light was coming in from above where I impacted the ship. There was a fire burning on the other side of the vessel, and there was an alien in there.

He was of the Nordic variety, dressed in what looked like your standard *When the Earth Stood Still* silver jumpsuit. That confused me. I wasn't expecting anything I found to represent a decades old Hollywood representation of an alien.

The alien had red blood covering the right side of his face and was off the couch. He appeared to be badly injured and was crawling away from the fire to the gash I was peering through. His eyes meet mine. They were blue and entirely human. I could see pain and fear and surprise in them.

He didn't draw a weapon or act in a threatening way. He seemed harmless and, frankly, pitiful. The fire behind him flared up. His eyes drilled into mine and he said one word. "Help."

I flashed back to the dead alien at Yellowstone. The

gaping hole in his chest caused by my neutrino bolt. I felt the guilt and revulsion that came with that memory. I knew this creature was my enemy, the enemy of my planet, but I couldn't leave it there to burn to death. I didn't think I could live with the guilt.

"Stay there," I said to him. "I'm going to have to burn my way through."

He nodded and backed up, cowering against the chair.

I gripped each side of the gap and pulled. I kept my reaction low and just tried to widen the gap so I could get through. It wouldn't budge. The metal was thin and strong.

I carefully increased my reaction in both hands the same way I had done when I was cutting through the safe. I plunged them into the metal at chest height and began cutting a wider opening into the ship. This metal was tough, much tougher than the steel safe I had just cut through. It was work, and I did my best to keep the bulk of my neutrino reaction low; I didn't want to radiate the alien to death.

I took several minutes to cut through. I watched as the fire spread towards the alien, its yellow tongues licking at the grey chair she hid behind. I hadn't realized it at first, but the alien was a female. She was thin and tall like the male versions I had seen, but with delicate feminine features and long blond hair pulled back.

As I neared the end of my cutting, she was in the fetal position, the chair above her fully on fire, the ship thick with smoke. I thought I heard her weeping.

I pulled away the metal I had cut through and yelled, "Come on, get out of there."

She was still in the fetal position and coughing. She looked at me and nodded. She tried to stand, but collapsed in pain. It looked like her leg was injured.

I let go of my neutrino form and crawled through the hole. The smoke was thick and acrid. It burned my eyes and my lungs and I began coughing. The floor of the vessel was a shiny metal. It seemed like I should have slid on it, but I didn't. The material provided excellent traction.

"Take my hand," I said in between coughs. I wasn't all the way in the ship, just far enough to reach her. The chair was completely on fire and being naked, I didn't want to get too close.

She grasped my hand with surprising strength and I pulled. I heard a sharp beeping noise coming from the ship followed by words in a language I had never heard. Her eyes meet mine and she coughed out, "Hurry!" I wasn't sure what was happening, but her urgency was clear and palpable.

I reached back and grabbed the edge of the ragged hole I had created and pulled hard. The metal was still hot and burned my hand.

The beeping noise became more insistent as I pulled her from the ship. It was clear she couldn't walk so I leaned down and got her over my shoulders in a firemen's carry and started moving forward as fast as I could. The ground beneath my bare feet was rough and cold, but I ignored it. My hand screamed with the pain of the fresh burn, but that didn't matter.

The beeping coming from the burning vessel behind us became louder and more insistent. I forced my legs into a jog. "Hurry," she grunted as I jogged along. I forced myself to move faster, my foot grazing a small prickly pear cactus as I moved, its needles biting into my flesh.

The beeping was so fast now, it was a continuous tone. "Down!" she yelled. I got the message, roughly tossing her to the ground. I stood, took a step back towards the burning ship, and changed back to my neutrino form. We were only about fifteen yards away, and if the ship was going to explode, that wasn't far enough.

I crouched down and extended both hands in front of me towards the ship, like I had done in the Verde Valley when the meteorites were descending on Lightningirl and me. This wasn't something I had practiced, and I didn't know if it would work, but I wanted to preserve the life of the alien if I could.

As the ship erupted into an orange ball of flame, a column of yellow light shot out of my chest and formed a shield in front of us. The fireball was quickly upon us, but the shield held, the explosion dividing around my shield.

It was quickly over. The ground all around us was burnt and blackened, the two of us in a small unscathed space. The ship was gone, nothing more than a few hunks of melted metal. I changed back to my biological form and went back to the alien. She was breathing and gave me a wan smile. I again wished that I had some medical training. I had no idea what to do. She didn't seem to be actively bleeding so I just smiled back. "You're going to be okay, help is on the way."

I studied the blast radius. The ship crashed about twenty yards north of the train tracks and the radius of the blast was about fifty yards. The charred ground around us was completely decimated. Even the rocks seemed to be mis-shaped as if the blast had melted them.

In the distance, to the east, I heard a train headed our way. I looked down at the rocks and wondered at this blast, how it had altered them.

I heard the train rumbling closer. It was a fair distance off, but I could hear it with my rat-enhanced hearing.

Melted rocks. Large blast area near the train tracks.

Train headed this way. It all tumbled together in my mind. "Oh, shit!" I said. I turned to the alien, "Hang in there, help is coming. I've got to go."

Chapter 13

Locomotive
Late Winter 2005, East of Flagstaff, Arizona

I FLEW FAST AND FOUND THE TRAIN. IT WAS A WESTBOUND Amtrak, just like the one we had just robbed, pulled by a silver locomotive with red, white, and blue stripes down the length of it.

I turned around, matched speed, and yelled through the little window on the side, "Stop this train. The tracks are out up ahead!"

There were two men inside. They both looked surprised to see me. I mean, of course they did. I was a flying yellow humanoid telling them to stop their train.

"Stop this train now!" I shouted.

The older one looked to the younger one and gave a nod. The younger one just stood there, his eyes wide, staring at me. The older one pushed him aside and started pressing buttons and pulling levers and the train started slowing, its metal wheels screeching and sparks flying. I flew up and a little ahead to get a better view. We only had a few hundred yards before the blast area, the train was going about seventy miles per hour and had no chance of stopping in time.

I looked back along the train—there were maybe fifty cars, all filled with passengers. If the train hit the blast area, it would derail, injuring and potentially killing many. I had to stop it.

I flew back to the front of the train and examined it. The top half was sloped with two windows. The bottom half was vertical with a big metal coupler sticking out. That seemed to be the sturdiest part. I carefully landed on it and lowered myself onto it so my back was facing the train.

It was a dizzying view, the tracks whizzing beneath my feet. I extended my feet and started thrusting. Slowly at first. I did my best to control my reaction so all the power was coming out of my feet. I didn't want to melt the coupling down.

The train was slowing, but still not fast enough. I added thrust from my hands and increased the thrust from my feet. The pressure of my thrust was holding me in place while my hands and feet were positioned straight ahead spewing columns of yellow.

The tracks beneath me were slowing noticeably, but it still wasn't going to be enough. I noticed that I was closer to the locomotive now, the coupling was melting under the heat of my reaction. I had no choice, I redoubled my efforts.

I continued to ramp up the thrust slowly. I didn't want to derail the train. I pointed the neutrino jets up a bit, so I wouldn't take out the tracks in front of us. I heard the squeal of the brakes increase and looked ahead noticing that the blast zone was now visible. The train tracks were there, but looked like melted plastic. Some of the railroad ties were on fire.

I thrusted more, I was now pressed directly against the

front edge of the train, molten metal splashing down on the tracks as the metal I was pressing against melted.

The force I was exerting against the train was tremendous, but the train was massively heavy and had a large amount of momentum that I was fighting.

The train had slowed to a few miles per hour, but the blast area was just ahead. I gave it everything I had, a cry escaping me as the effort took its toll.

I felt the metal that pressed against my back give way and I was completely engulfed by the train. I saw sparks as I melted through electrical systems and heard the squeal and groan of metal as my thrust continued to burrow me farther into the engine.

I stopped thrusting. I didn't know much about how a locomotive was designed, but I did know they ran on diesel fuel and I didn't want to cause an explosion.

I quickly crawled forward to the front of the train just as it reached the damaged section of the tracks. The train was barely at a crawl as its front wheels came off the track and burrowed into the freshly charred earth. The train ground to a halt, the locomotive's back wheels staying on the track.

I breathed a sigh of relief and flew back to where the alien was. As I walked to the spot, about fifty yards from where the train had stopped, I had this fear that she would be gone. That by stopping the train I had given up our chance to find out why the aliens wanted us dead. I could almost hear Toxicwasteman admonishing me for not letting the collateral damage happen, for not focusing on the larger mission, the greater good.

Fortunately, my fear was unfounded. She was still there, her eyes open and staring at me and the train beyond. Her eyes were wide as she watched me approach.

"Are you okay?" I asked.

She nodded slowly. It was a strange nod, stiff and awkward as if she had to think about the gesture. As if it wasn't normal for her. "You are unexpected," she said.

I wasn't sure what she meant. Was my presence unexpected, or my actions? "My name is Nik," I said. "What's yours?"

She grimaced in pain and took a deep breath and told me her name. I had no chance of repeating it. It began with a "sh" sound and had a rolling "r" in it (as well as several clicks and way too many vowels).

"Oh, I'll never be able to say that," I said. "How about Sarah? Do you mind if I call you Sarah?"

"No, Sarah is good," she said.

I smiled and turned to the west where I heard the sound of an approaching helicopter. Help was coming, but I really wasn't sure how helpful they would be.

Chapter 14

An Alien Named Sarah
Late Winter 2005, East of Flagstaff, Arizona

WE ONLY HAD A MINUTE OR TWO BEFORE THE HELICOPTER arrived. Before the military swept in and took over. I let my neutrino form go and walked closer to the alien, squatting down.

"Why?" I asked. "Why are you here? Why are you trying to kill us?" I hugged my arms around me as the cold bit at my skin. I could hear the helicopter coming closer and the sounds of shouting from the train behind me. "Please, what have we done?"

"It's not what you have done," she said slowly. "It is what you will do."

"Are you from the future?" I asked.

A bark escaped her chest. It took me a moment to realize that it was a laugh. "No. Time travel not possible. I did not speak correctly. It is what probability says you will do." She groaned and clutched her abdomen. "I should not speak," she said through gritted teeth. "Is not my place."

I heard the helicopter land behind me. I tried to get her to tell me more, but she would not speak of it.

THE MILITARY PERSONNEL FIRST ON SITE WERE ARMY National Guard from Camp Navaho, about thirty miles away. They created a perimeter around the wreckage, the alien, and myself. The train tracks were a few miles away from I-40 at this point and only some poorly maintained dirt roads led back here. I could hear sirens in the distance from the approaching emergency services personnel. We had a train wreck, a crashed alien spacecraft, and a live alien all in one spot. This place was about to become a circus.

A young sergeant by the name of Mills seemed to be in charge. He had been kind enough to loan me his jacket so I would not completely freeze. But, he hadn't produced a medic yet.

"She's dying," I said, not for the first time.

"I am sorry, sir," Mills said, "we didn't bring a medic with us. One is in route." He was around thirty, stocky, with a square jaw and grey eyes.

"You said that ten minutes ago."

"Yes sir," he replied, "And I'll say it again next time you ask."

I smiled and almost laughed. He was right. I was being a pain, pacing back and forth, feeling helpless. Once again I was confronted with my helplessness in medical situations.

"What about first aid?" I asked. "Surely you have training in first aid."

He nodded, "Yes sir, we do. But orders are to create a perimeter, contain the situation, and do not interact with the alien life-form."

I wasn't laughing anymore. "She's going to die without treatment." I looked over at her prone form. She was unconscious, her breathing shallow, and the last time I checked, her pulse weak. His gaze strayed to the alien and back to me again. "Do you have any idea how much more a live alien is worth than a dead one? Do you know what this might mean?"

He stood there, his face impassive. Of course he didn't know what this meant. He had no idea that the aliens were bent on the destruction of the human race.

"Sergeant Mills, please. Get someone over here with first aid training. This is on me. I'll take the heat for the decision."

"Sorry, sir," he said. "You are not part of my chain of command. You cannot take the heat for the decision. I will."

It was at times like this that I was glad that I was a civilian. Orders, it's all about orders for them, not what makes sense, not what is best. And to be fair, I understood the system. In battle you needed soldiers that took orders, not ones that questioned everything.

"Those orders are out of date," I said. "They didn't know the situation on the ground."

"Orders, sir," he said turning away from me.

I cursed under my breath and jogged towards the train, the rough ground cutting into my feet. One of the soldiers on the periphery yelled at me to stop, but I ignored him. I was a civilian. I was going to do what I thought best.

As I approached the train, a fair number of people had deboarded and were milling about, looking my way. Well, considering my state of dress, they could have been staring at me, but I think it was the silver wreckage of the spaceship and the military personnel that caught their attention. Not that I didn't draw some stares. I was wearing a grey camouflage military coat, with my bare white legs and feet showing below it as I gingerly jogged towards them.

"Is there a doctor here?" I shouted. "We've got an injured

woman over there. She needs immediate attention. Doctor? Is anyone a doctor?"

They all stared at me. They probably thought I was crazy, running in my bare feet, barely dressed. And then whispering started and rippled through the crowd. A young girl towards the front pointed at me and said, "He's Neutrinoman!" The quality of stares changed then. From pure suspicion to wonder and some fear.

"Please," I said, "I need a doctor. It is urgent."

I heard someone say, "I'm a doctor," but couldn't see him. Soon an older man shouldered his way through the crowd. He was short and round with greying hair, round glasses, and kind brown eyes. "I'm Doctor Romero, what's the problem?"

"Thank God," I said. At this point the cell phones were out taking pictures and video of me and the wreckage. I walked towards him and took his elbow, gently pulling him forward. "There is a woman, badly injured. I am afraid she is going to die. Can you help?"

He nodded as we started our way back.

"I AM SORRY, SIR," THE SOLIDER SAID. "I CANNOT ALLOW a civilian through."

I studied him. He was tall, lanky, young, and looked scared. They only had enough personnel so that each soldier was guarding about twenty yards of the perimeter. The soldiers on either side were eying us.

"He's a doctor," I said. "The woman over there needs medical attention."

"I am sorry, sir, orders."

My anger was growing, about to boil over into fury. A life

was at stake, a doctor was needed. It was really that simple. "Do you know who I am?" I asked. The solider nodded his head. "Then you know what I am capable of. Out of my way, son. I don't want to hurt you." I felt silly calling him "son," I was maybe six or seven years older than him, but I was trying to establish some kind of authority.

He looked truly terrified. I felt bad about it, but what could I do? He stood there staring at me and I yelled, "Now!" He stepped aside and I pulled Dr. Romero forward.

"Look," I whispered to the doctor, "do you trust me?"

He nodded, his eyes wide.

"We are going to meet more resistance," I began. "I am going to have to play the only card I can. What I need you to do is go to her and keep her alive. The fate of our planet may just rest in your hands, my friend."

He pushed his glasses up onto his nose, his eyes widening as he nodded. Once again, I felt silly invoking such language, "the fate of our planet," and such. But this was turning into a huge drama and I needed the alien to survive. Looking back, I am not sure what gave me such certainty that day, but I am glad I acted on it.

"Don't be surprised, but I am going to turn into Neutrinoman soon. Don't listen to anyone but me. Your objective is to keep that woman alive no matter what. Understand?"

He nodded, licking his lips. Sergeant Mills and two other soldiers were on their way to intercept us.

"I need to leave you now," I said pushing him forward. "Go straight to her, listen to no one but me. Now, run!" He ran towards the woman, while I ran directly towards Mills. I summoned forth my neutrino form. After one step the coat was smoldering, after two steps, it was on fire and I was flying, five seconds later I stood between Mills and

Dr. Romero in my full neutrino form, the coat continuing to burn its way off of me. I heard shouts from the crowd gathered back by the train.

I held my hand out, palm forward. "You will not interfere with the doctor."

"I have orders," Mills said, the soldiers next to him pointing their rifles at me.

"And you have done your best to fulfill them. Now, stand down. I don't want to see any of you hurt."

Interview, Part 4

Late Winter 2005, WNN Studios, Los Angeles

I LEARNED AN IMPORTANT LESSON THAT DAY WITH DIANE Madison. It's not like it was a new thing, or that I hadn't heard it before. But then and there under the hot lights of the studio, on live TV with hundreds of millions of people watching, I learned an important lesson: your opponent's home turf is not the place to make a stand.

Obvious, right?

"We're back on *Real Life with Diane Madison*, today we are talking with none other than Neutrinoman," she said to the camera before turning to me. "So Nik, I was thinking over the break. Maybe there are some skeptics out there, some folks who might doubt that you are who you say you are. You know, real people who know what can be done with a special effects budget today."

Was she going to suggest... she couldn't. "There was no special effects there, Diane," I said.

"Well, just to reassure the few that are still in doubt, maybe you could do an in-studio demonstration." Her smile was innocent, but her eyes were hard. This is what she meant by "Let's play."

"I'm sorry, Diane, but I am not safe to be around when I transform into Neutrinoman," I said.

She nodded thoughtfully. "I have heard—and you can tell me if this is true—that it is possible for you to do a partial transformation. Maybe you can do that for us."

"While it's possible, it is quite difficult." I didn't want to do it. If people believed, they believed. Those that doubted my existence, and still doubt my existence, weren't going to be fooled by something done on live TV. I mean, didn't some magician make the Washington Monument disappear on live TV?

"Please," she said with a smile, "for those real people out there. Just a brief, unplanned demonstration."

I nodded, placing my left elbow on the glass desk and pointing my index finger up. I concentrated, slowly transforming the tip of my finger. It went from normal flesh to a glowing, swirling yellow. I looked at Diane and a trace of flickering yellow light illumined her. She had a look of awe and wonder on her face, like a young girl coming downstairs on Christmas morning to a tree with a stack of presents underneath.

I believed that look, I thought it was genuine. It's what inspired me to do what I did next. My motives were not pure. She had maneuvered me into this. I was hoping to do something that would make her regret doing that. I slowly moved my glowing fingertip to the top of her desk and placed it to the glass there.

It melted and glowed where I touched. I slowly moved my finger up, and then down and to the right diagonally and then up again, forming an "N." I then continued on drawing a circle that started at the top right of the "N" and looped around stopping just before the bottom right corner.

While I did this, a cameraman came in close and filmed the whole thing. The glass glowed a bright yellow-orange and moved aside like I was dragging my finger through honey. He stayed there filming it after I was done, as the glow slowly faded and the glass cooled.

I looked up and Diane was beaming at me, slowly nodding her head. I was hoping I was doing something she didn't like, but I had done exactly what she wanted. She would take my feeble attempt at thwarting her and use it to advance her career. That desk, branded by me, by Neutrinoman, would be part of her shows for the rest of her career. My little act of defiance had reinforced our link. The last thing I had wanted to do.

"And we're clear," I heard the voice say.

"That was perfect," Diane said to me. "Just perfect. As if we had rehearsed it. The two of us are quite the team."

Chapter 15

A Changed Man

Late Winter 2005, East of Flagstaff, Arizona

WE HAD AN UNEASY TRUCE. I WAS PACING, IN MY NEUTRINO form, in a circle around Dr. Romero and the alien. Sergeant Mills and several of his soldiers were positioned in a loose circle around my circle.

I looked at the doctor and the alien. He had propped her legs up with his jacket and applied some makeshift bandages. "I need a first aid kit," he said to me. "Something. What she needs is a hospital, but even a first aid kit would help."

I nodded to Dr. Romero and walked to Sergeant Mills. I stopped when I was about five yards away, my neutrino reaction low. "Can you get the doctor a first aid kit?" I asked. He didn't answer, so I continued. "Look, she's dying. You have to understand how valuable she is alive. We are facing a threat we don't comprehend, a threat we need to learn everything we can about. We've never had this opportunity before. Please, help me."

His eyes flicked from me to Sarah and back again before he nodded and shouted at one of the soldiers who went running to the helicopter and then ran back to the doctor with a large first aid kit.

As I watched I had this uneasy feeling. I was embarrassed. I knew what I was doing was the right thing. I had no doubt about it. But the means I was employing didn't feel quite right. I didn't tell the doctor what he was getting into. I didn't tell him I needed him to treat an alien—although with the wrecked craft and her odd dress, he might have figured it out by now. I bullied and threatened a soldier to get the doctor and me through. And just then I had left out my main real reason for wanting to save the alien: my own guilt over the one I had killed in Wyoming. The vision of that alien with its burnt chest still haunted me.

"Thank you," I said to Mills as I continued my perimeter walk over the blackened and blasted earth, praying that this time the alien would survive.

COLONEL WILLIAMS WAS FURIOUS, HIS GREEN EYES flashing. I expected him to be, but the volume of it caught me off guard.

"Who the hell do you think you are, Nichols?" he yelled as he approached me. His face was red and his hands were balled into fists. He was dressed in camo-wear, pants, and a winter jacket. I watched as the rest of the personnel spilled forth from the three Huey helicopters. "You have interfered with my orders. You brought a civilian into this situation and you have bullied soldiers. Who the hell do you think you are?"

I took a breath and considered my words. What I wanted to say was, "I am Neutrinoman and once you start giving better orders, I won't have to interfere with them." But I didn't say that. I knew what I wanted, and I knew that wouldn't get me there.

"I'm sorry, Colonel," I said, as I let my neutrino form go and stood naked in front of him. "The alien was dying, I had to do something." I gestured to the alien and Dr. Romero behind me. I was glad to see two medics jogging towards her with several large cases. "We need her, Colonel." Again I marveled at how much I left out. At how I didn't assign the blame for my actions on him, although it would have been easy. I was being who I needed to be to get what I wanted. It occurred to me then that the time I spent with Tom Tyree had rubbed off. And that thought was terrifying.

His mouth was opened, as if to fire off a retort, but my words seemed to disarm his anger. He brushed at his short salt-and-pepper hair, nodded, and yelled to no one in particular, "Someone bring this man a blanket or a coat!"

THEY STABILIZED SARAH AND LOADED HER INTO ONE OF the helicopters. Dr. Romero, Colonel Williams, two medics, the pilot, and I were also in the helicopter.

I sat there wrapped in a scratchy blanket, watching the alien, watching Sarah. She was sleeping and looked peaceful and not at all alien. Her head was properly bandaged and her abdomen was bandaged. The medics hovered over her and Dr. Romero sat next to me looking scared.

"I'm sorry I got you into this," I yelled, so he could hear me over the sound of the helicopter.

He shrugged, but it didn't set my mind at ease. He was trying to be relaxed in his body language, but his eyes told a different story. At this point I am sure he had heard enough to know that Sarah was not normal.

"I'll get you back to your life as soon as I can," I said.

He smiled. It was a fleeting twitch of his lips, soon replaced by a worried frown.

THE HELICOPTER FLEW US TO LUKE AIR FORCE BASE. Sarah was rushed into surgery, and I was rushed into a debrief session with Colonel Williams and General Marcus. Marcus had been flown in to deal with the alien.

I won't go into details about the debrief, except to say it was long and exhausting and I was irritated enough that I gave them the alternate GPS coordinates for LoVE's lair. It felt wrong to me to lie to them like that. I didn't like it. But the thought of having access to that uranium ore was just too much. I had to keep it to myself.

There is one aspect of it that is worth recounting, though. They were rather puzzled as to why I called Licia after Tom Tyree and the gang had left me next to the wreckage of the alien ship.

"Why did you call Ms. Lopez first?" General Marcus asked. Marcus is somewhere in his sixties, looking like he was once fit but carrying about fifty extra pounds. He had snow-white hair and blue-green eyes.

"Were you never young, General?" I replied with a weary smile.

He paused, his eyes going distant, before he said, "I was never *that* young, son." And then realization dawned on his face. "Are you and Ms. Lopez..." he looked at Colonel Williams. "Are they?"

"According to Ms. Lopez," Williams said, "they are not."

"It's complicated," I offered.

"Well, it's inappropriate," General Marcus said. "The

stakes are high, son. You need to have a clear head when you are out there, not get distracted by... by..."

"By a contained electrical reaction in the shape of a beautiful woman," I said.

"Yes, that," he agreed with a nod of his head.

"Too late, sir," I said. "The damage is done."

The conversation went on from there. It was like the lecture a father would give to his teenage son. It was just as clichéd, and just as effective (which is to say, not at all).

Well, it was effective, but not in the way Marcus and Williams intended. They were hoping to dissuade me from my romantic pursuit of Licia. They used logic and reason. It was laughably ineffective. I was in the throes of passion and romance, how is logic and reason going to contend with that? What was effective was diverting the discussion to my love life. While it wasn't fun or comfortable, they forgot to dig further into why I called Licia first and not them when Tom and company departed.

As the debrief went on, I marveled at how I was continuing to manipulate those around me. I was shocked at how easy it was. I had watched Tom do it and somehow that had jumped to me like some contagious virus. My motives, of course, were much more pure than his (or so I told myself), so the manipulation was justified.

The truth was I called Licia first to give Tom and company time to get away. Tom had successfully convinced me that they were going to be needed in the coming days as we fought the alien threat.

As I write this from my current perspective and think back to that time when Tom Tyree tried to recruit me into LoVE, I realize that this shift in my personality was his intention the whole time. He wasn't trying to recruit me;

he was trying to prepare me—in his own twisted way—for what was to come.

And that meant giving me a power supply independent from the military and a willingness to manipulate people to get what I believed in. It also meant sowing seeds of doubt in my mind as to the capability of the military to wage this war.

He infected me. He changed me. I'm not sure what would have happened if he hadn't.

Chapter 16

The Right Thing to Do

Late Winter 2005, Luke Air Force Base, Arizona

GENERAL MARCUS LOOKED LIKE HE HAD JUST EATEN A lemon. His round face was pinched and sour looking, his cheeks flushed. "The alien won't talk to us," he said. We had been at Luke Air Force base for two days, a boring stretch of debriefs, medical exams, and waiting around.

"Okay," I said with a shrug. My disinterest was feigned. There was obviously something going on. I sat in a small conference room reviewing the statement and other documents that had been produced by my debrief. I turned back to the laptop I was working on.

Marcus cleared his throat and I looked up.

"It says it will only talk to you," he said, his face puckering even more.

I wanted to lecture him. To tell him that if he thought of the alien as a "she" instead of an "it," or, better yet, thought of her as "Sarah," maybe he would get better results. Instead I said, "How can I help, General?"

"Son," he began, "I need you to talk to her. I need you to find out what she knows. I..." His voice trailed off and his face fell. I could see the bluster and energy just draining from him. He suddenly wasn't a hard-ass, but a chubby, scared kid. I didn't want to, but I felt for him. We were up against an unknown enemy of unknown power with unknown motivations. This wasn't the kind of war we had ever fought.

"I'll talk to her," I said.

His blue-green eyes met mine and he nodded sharply. "Thank you," he said as he pushed himself into a standing position. He stood up straight and all the bluster came flowing back in. "Our people will be right in and get you ready for your time with the alien." With that, he turned and left.

Two other officers entered as he was leaving, and they spent the next four hours telling me what I could and couldn't say around her, what I could and couldn't do, and what information I was to try to get and how I was to get that information.

I let all the crap flow in one ear and out the other. No wonder she wasn't talking to them. It was early evening when they escorted me in to see her.

"HI, SARAH," I SAID WHEN I ENTERED THE ROOM. WE were in the infirmary in a small hospital room. It looked just like the one I awoke in after taking on the asteroid the aliens hurtled at us. There was one significant difference. She was strapped to the bed at her wrists and ankles, like some mental patient they were afraid might try to hurt herself.

She smiled weakly. It was a totally human gesture, and totally disarming. "Hello," she answered.

I was at a loss as to what to say. There was a guard right outside the door and several cameras watching our every move. This wasn't a private conversation, although I wished it was. I walked over to her bed and undid the Velcro strap on her left wrist. I didn't really think it through, I just acted. The restraint seemed excessive. She wasn't going to go anywhere. She smiled a "thank you" at me as her hand went to her face, probing the bandages on her forehead, and then to her abdomen. She grimaced, her hand finding mine as she pulled me close.

Her breath was warm and smelled a little rotten, like someone who hadn't brushed their teeth for way too long. "Free me and I will help," she said very quietly, her exhalation tickling my ear.

"Help?" I whispered back.

"I am nobody, but my people will listen if I speak. They have to. For you I will speak."

"Speak?" I didn't understand what she was telling me.

"None have done so, none will" she continued. "But for you I will. I am enemy, you saved me. You saved train. You are worth speaking for."

I turned and looked as I heard a shout from the hallway and the sound of running feet. I assumed that they could hear us and that wasn't sitting very well. I turned back to Sarah. "Please," she said, "let me go. I am nobody, but I will speak."

Her words were strange. I didn't know exactly what she meant, but I believed her. I let go of her hand and moved to the door. I needed more time. The door opened and Colonel Williams was standing there, breathing heavily, his face flush from exertion.

I folded my arms across my chest, blocking him. "Do you trust me, Colonel?" I asked. His eyes were focused on the alien behind me, not me. "Colonel," I repeated loudly, "do you trust me?"

His eyes met mine and he nodded once.

"Then please give us a few minutes."

His eyes narrowed and he looked at Sarah then back to me. "Make it quick, Marcus is on his way." With that he stepped back and closed the door.

"I DID NOT SEND YOU IN THERE TO HAVE A PRIVATE CON-versation, to hold hands with it," Marcus yelled, his round face red. "I sent you in there to gather intelligence. I sent you in there to talk sense into it. To find out why the hell the aliens are here and why the hell they want us dead. I sent you in there to..." he trailed off, the anger fading and his shoulders stooping.

He pulled up a chair and sat across from me in the con-ference room. It was the one I had been debriefed in earlier.

"What were you thinking?" he asked quietly.

I looked down, my eyes wandering across the warm wood of the table. What had I been thinking? The truth was I hadn't been. I had been running on instinct. I had been doing what I thought was right. "We need to let her go," I said.

His eyes widened and his face reddened. He pushed back his chair noisily and stood again. "What?" he asked.

"We need to let her go," I repeated.

"Son, this is the best break we've gotten so far. Why in the blue blazes would I want to let her go?"

"If you let her go," I said, "she will help us."

"Help us? How the hell is she going to help us? She's a pilot of some sort, maybe the equivalent of an officer, but not someone who can help us."

"She will speak," I said. I knew it sounded silly, that I sounded like her, but I didn't know how else to put it. Because in truth I didn't know exactly what she meant. I just knew it felt like the right thing.

"Speak? What the hell is that supposed to mean?"

"That is what she said. I think it means that she will advocate for us. Speak on our behalf."

"But she's nobody, son. She's a pilot, who's going to listen to her?"

"I don't know," I said with a shrug. "But you know what, General? I am a janitor and here you are listening to me."

He sat heavily in his chair, a noisy sigh escaping him. We talked about this for the next thirty minutes, but in the end he refused.

After he left, I sat there alone in that room trying to talk myself out of what seemed to be the next thing to do. What seemed to be the right thing to do.

You know those stories about the heroes who act courageously and are never plagued by doubt? Well, this is not one of those stories. While I am blessed to know my own mind, to have a sense of right and wrong, a moral compass if you will, I am also plagued by doubt.

And really, I think we all are. Or we all should be. For example, Tom Tyree has a strong sense of his destiny, of what it is he should do. But, he doesn't have a shred of doubt. He is not assailed by worry or concerned about consequences. He is free to act without all the weight of doubt. And that is what makes him dangerous.

Me, sitting there alone in that small conference room, with its bland black chairs and its boring white walls, I was assailed by doubt and fear. I had conviction. I was convinced that we needed to free the alien. That she would "speak" for us, and somehow that would be a good thing. But I didn't know if I had the courage to do it. I didn't know if I could do it in a way that I could live with.

So, what is a man to do when he is plagued with doubt? Call the woman he is trying to woo, of course, and lay it all on the line.

That is what I did, but that is not how I arrived there. My calling her really had nothing to do with wooing her and had everything to do with wanting her level head and capable presence.

I used the phone in the conference room. I am guessing the caller ID probably said "Luke AFB," or something like that, because she picked up right away.

"Hello?" she said.

"Licia, it's Nik. I need your help." I launched right in. No "I miss you," "you complete me," or any of the other romantic stuff that was going through my head. And she responded.

"Is everything okay?" she asked.

"No," I answered. "I really need your help, and it's not something I can speak of on the phone. Can you come here?"

There was a slight pause. I was afraid she would refuse. But she said, "Of course. I'll meet you by the power lines. Southwest corner in thirty minutes. Please bring a robe."

Interview, Part 5

Late Winter 2005, WNN Studios, Los Angeles

THAT SYMBOL I BURNED INTO DIANE MADISON'S DESK, the N-circle, stuck. The next week I saw pictures of people in T-shirts with it emblazed on the chest. It had been stylized, and was done in neutrino-yellow, but the N-circle symbol started showing up everywhere.

It was puzzling to me. I know, I know, I was a real life superhero, but that doesn't mean that I was prepared for the fame of it. I had been trying, quite unsuccessfully, to mess with Diane Madison. I hadn't expected to brand myself. Or to brand Lightningirl, for that matter.

A few days after the N-circle symbol started showing up, I read one of those fluff entertainment pieces on it. In it they had a picture of a young woman with one of the T-shirts on. Except the symbol had been altered, it had been rotated ninety degrees to the right. The N looked like a Z, and the Z kind of looked like a lightning bolt. One symbol, two superheroes.

And that's the thing about life. You never know the moments that are really going to change things, do you?

THE INTERVIEW WAS DECIDEDLY UNCOMFORTABLE. NOT because her questions were hard, they had been provided beforehand and I had been coached extensively. What was hard was knowing millions were watching. Knowing that everything I said would be picked apart and analyzed. Knowing how much rode on me saying the right thing in the right way.

Give me a meteor attack or an alien plot any day. Give me Tom Tyree and his band of psychopaths.

"How does it feel," Diane asked, "to have so much power? To be able to do so much good?"

I smiled a weary smile. "It's a burden," I began, "that's for sure. That whole Spider-Man saying—with great power comes great responsibility—is not far off. Except I would probably use some stronger adjectives. It's easy, much too easy, to harm with the power I wield, so I think about it all the time. I do my best to help much, much more than I harm." I paused, licking my lips. That was the answer I had been coached to give. What I added was off the script. "You must understand that, Diane. Behind that desk, you wield a lot of power, and that power can be used for good, or for ill. Surely you feel the responsibility of it."

She nodded gravely. "Believe me I do. We work hard here to make sure the stories we tell are what the American people need to hear. Sometimes they are hard to tell. Sometimes there are consequences to the telling. But if we don't believe in the story, we don't run it."

"Like when you revealed my identity to the world," I said. This wasn't the time or place, and I had promised myself I wouldn't say anything about it, but it just slipped out. The wound was just too fresh.

"Just like that," she said, her brow furrowed. "We knew it would have an impact on you and your family, but we felt strongly, we still feel strongly, in the need for transparency. From our government and from our heroes."

I wanted to say more, but I kept my mouth shut. I wanted to say that if she had known of the consequences, why didn't they warn us and our families, but it was finally becoming clear that in this venue, she was the master, she had the superpowers. Just stick to the script.

She paused, shuffling through the papers on her desk. "Let's start on a new topic. One that we at *Real Life* feel strongly needs to come out into the open. And that is the topic of aliens." She turned to me, her face grave. "Nik, can you confirm or deny the presence of an alien species on our planet that is intent on our destruction?"

This was it. This was, as far as the military was concerned, why I was here. It was time to start the public relations campaign. I took a deep breath nodded, and said, "I can confirm that, Diane."

Diane stared at me, blinking, her mouth opening and closing. She took a breath and turned to the camera. "Stay with us for more *Real Life with Diane Madison* where we will find out more about this alien threat."

After "clear" was yelled, she turned and smiled at me. "We're going to go a long way, you and I. A long, long way." I just smiled back. I was terrified.

Maybe she was just arrogant, she couldn't have known what would happen, but that statement certainly came true as the years unfolded.

Chapter 17

Speak for Us

Late Winter 2005, Luke Air Force Base, Arizona

I ROOTED AROUND AND FOUND A ROBE. I SAW COLONEL Williams on the way out and told him that I needed some air and was going for a run. He was about to say something, but I didn't give him a chance. I pushed past him and went out of the infirmary.

As you would imagine, an air force base has some serious power requirements. The power lines that ran into it were large enough for Lightningirl to travel on. Once I got outside, I jogged past a few drab buildings parallel to the dry, dusty runway to the southwest corner of the base. Luke is a big place, and the location was about a mile away. But at this point my aerobic capacity was improving, so it actually felt good.

I saw her coming in. A flash of light running along the power line and then a small lightning bolt stabbing from a transformer down to the ground, and then she was there.

She was so beautiful, so primal. Every time I see her like that I know that there is such a thing as a goddess, because she is one. I wanted to throw myself at her feet and beg for her love. I wanted to transform into Neutrinoman, sweep her up, and fly her out of here. I wanted to hold her hand and never let her go.

But I didn't do any of those things. I stopped a few feet in front of her, held the robe out, closed my eyes, and turned my head.

I could feel her transform from Lightningirl to Licia. One moment the hairs on my arm were standing straight up and I could smell ozone, and the next I felt her moving her biological body into the robe and I could smell her. I slowly inhaled taking just a moment to breathe in that scent. To let my olfactory senses break it down: clean and sterile, fresh, a trace of ozone, but still distinctively her. It was a subtle scent—much of what I smell from most people was left behind with her transformation. What was left was the something akin to the smell after a heavy monsoon.

"Okay," she said quietly.

I opened my eyes. She was wrapped in the white robe, her brown eyes meeting mine. "Thank you for coming," I said, swallowing every romantically clichéd phrase that was banging around my head.

"So what's going on?" she asked.

I told her. It came spilling out in an avalanche of words. I paced and gestured, letting my body express the emotions I was feeling, stopping only when a jet passing overhead drowned me out.

I didn't hold back, I didn't edit, I didn't worry about how I sounded. I trusted her so it was okay to be passionate, to be stumbling on my words, to appear foolish. It was Licia, so I could be me.

GENERAL MARCUS LOOKED UNCOMFORTABLE. HE WAS fidgeting in his seat and kept flipping through the papers in front of him. Colonel Williams was there as well as several other people. They were dressed in military uniforms, but I think they were lawyers.

After I had said my piece, Licia marched me back and demanded a meeting with Marcus and Williams.

She had changed and was dressed in scrubs as she paced the length of the little conference room. I was sitting across from Marcus and Williams, my stomach tight and my palms sweating.

"Let's start over," Licia said, stopping at the head of the table and leaning against it. "General, Nik is resolved that this alien, this 'Sarah,' be released. Nik, the general is just as resolved to keep her, to question her, to use her to help us learn about this threat." She took a deep breath and sighed heavily. "We need to find a middle ground, gentlemen."

"With all due respect, Mr. Nichols," the general said. "There is a chain of command for a reason. This decision comes from above me. It is imperative that we find out more about these aliens. It makes no sense to let her go."

"With all due respect, General," I countered. "I am not part of the military. I brought down the ship she was flying. I injured her. I saved her. And I feel responsible for her. She wants to help us. We need to let her try."

"I don't think you're qualified to make that kind of—" the general began.

"Because I'm not drinking the same Kool-Aid you all are?" I said, cutting him off. "Because I'm a dumb janitor who stumbled into power. Because..." The argument escalated from there until the general and I were both standing up yelling at each other across the table.

After a minute of this, two tiny lightning bolts stabbed out from Licia's outstretched hand and hit Marcus and me in the chest. He looked shocked, I'm sure it didn't feel good to him, but I liked it. In both cases it got us to shut up.

"Here's what's going to happen if you two don't figure this out," Licia said, her voice low and dangerous. "Nik here is going to do something stupid. He's going to try to break her out of here. He's going to try to get me to help him. And if I refuse him, he will find other help." I opened my mouth to speak but she held up her hand stopping me and turned to the general. "And when he does, you are going to attempt to use force to stop him. Who prevails in this conflict doesn't matter. We all lose. The government loses Neutrinoman, and Neutrinoman loses his support system. And then our defeat by the aliens is assured." She paused and sighed wearily. "Now sit down and talk to each other."

"HI, SARAH," I SAID AS WE ENTERED THE HOSPITAL ROOM. General Marcus, Colonel Williams, and Licia were with me. "Can we talk?"

She looked at the uniforms the men were wearing, a look of fear on her face, and then back to me. "You. I will talk with you."

"Thank you, Sarah," I said. I pulled a stool up to her bed and everyone else stayed back a few paces. They had put her restraints back on. I took them off and asked, "How are you feeling today?"

"Getting stronger," she said as she pushed herself up in the bed. Her blond hair was dirty and clung to her face. The room smelled of chemicals and she needed to bathe. It was some comfort to me that aliens smelled the same way we did. "But that matters not. I don't matter. Will you release me?" Her eyes wandered to those standing behind me and back to me.

"I want to. I am trying to convince them it is the right thing to do. But, I need your help, Sarah. I need you to explain to us what you mean when you told me you would 'speak' for us."

She looked confused, but said, "Speak. It is... the word is not good, not right. But you don't have the right word. No one has spoken for you, so anyone can speak. If you let me go I will speak and they will listen."

"They?" Williams asked. "Do you mean your leaders?"

She nodded. "Yes. I am no one, but no one can speak and all will listen. It is..." she trailed off, her brow furrowed. "It is law."

"What will you speak?" Marcus asked.

"I will speak of him," she said nodding towards me. "I will tell how he saved me, saved others, tries to help me now. I am no one. I have nothing. But the yellow one helps."

"Will that change anything?" Licia asked. She stepped forward. I could feel her right behind me, small tendrils of energy passing between our bodies. I focused on Sarah and tried to ignore it. Sarah's eyebrows rose as she noticed the interaction. "Will that stop the attacks?"

"Yes," she said. "Maybe for a short time, maybe for all time, but attack will stop. When I speak they will listen. All will discuss. All will decide."

I turned to General Marcus and saw him nodding.

Chapter 18

Laying It on the Line
Late Winter 2005, Luke Air Force Base, Arizona

"THANK YOU," I SAID TO LICIA. WE HAD WALKED SILENTLY to the high-tension power lines.

She smiled—it was genuine, but not pure. I'm sure she was happy at the outcome, but the undercurrents of emotions she was feeling almost overwhelmed the smile. "You are welcome, Nik. Thank you for trusting me enough to call. Especially, since... you know..."

"Don't you see it?" I asked. "What a great team we are? How we are meant to be together?" I raised my hand until it was close enough to her that the yellow tendril of neutronic energy stabbed out from my body to hers while the white tendril of electricity jumped from her body to mine.

"Nik, please. Don't."

"I know, I know, you are not the romantic type. You are practical, sensible, worried that my feelings for you will make me stupid."

She folded her arms and said, "It's not that simple and you know it."

"Well then, explain it to me."

She sighed. "What's at risk here is all of humanity, Nik. We can't get distracted by feelings. We have to stay focused. We have to be able to work together, follow orders, do what we need to do."

I smiled, which seemed to confuse her. "So, you do have feelings for me."

"That's not the point."

"Not the point?" I asked. "Seriously? There is no other point. This world is on the brink. We are on the front lines of this war—which hopefully we are about to get a break from—and life is more uncertain than ever. Don't you see? It's so hard to find love and in the midst of this q-morph, alien madness we've found it. It's right here. We can't turn our backs on it."

"Nik... please, don't."

I was wound up now, the words rushing forth. I couldn't stop myself. "You worry about the decisions I will make if we are a couple and fighting together. That I'll somehow lose my mind because you are there and sacrifice the world for you." I paused and chuckled rather lamely. "But you are what I am fighting for, whether we are a couple or not."

"Me?"

"Not you exactly, but what you represent."

"I don't understand."

"I am fighting for this world and the people I love and all the things I love about it. I am fighting for desert sunsets, where the dust in the air makes the sky glow orange. I am fighting for my parents and my friends so they can lead their lives without these kinds of worries. I am fighting for Super Bowl Sunday and Thanksgiving, New Years, and bad sci-fi. I am fighting for love, because that is what it all comes down to. The people I love and the things they love. And you know what, Licia? You represent love for me. Whether you want to or not. You represent what I want the most, what I have always wanted the most, and that is what I fight for. I fight for you." I felt myself slouch as the words abated. I was drained emotionally. Her eyes glistened with tears, but I knew it wasn't enough.

"You are so romantic," she said, her hand brushing at my shoulder. "I do love that about you. But it's not enough, Nik. We have to keep our heads on. We have to be practical. If we survive this, then we can entertain the romantic. But, for now, we must stay grounded in the practical." She stepped back so our bodies were no longer interacting. I missed it.

"Practical?" I asked.

"Yes, practical."

"Okay, I'll give you practical." I stepped closer until the tendrils of energy started to jump from skin to skin. "We are meant to be together. Not in some romantic sense, but quite literally." I moved closer and the exchange intensified. "Our bodies know each other. We are stronger together than we are apart. And we are a team. Like it or not, the military will be using us as a team because it's obvious. I couldn't have taken down that asteroid without you. Do you agree?"

She nodded slowly.

"We need to know each other—our quirks, our habits. The better we know each other the better we can work together, the more powerful we will become. In short, intimacy. We are partners in this fight, and if we are partners emotionally, romantically, then we will be better able to meet this challenge, to rely on each other to survive."

Her eyebrows came together and she blinked rapidly as tears began to run down her cheeks. She opened her mouth and shook her head, her eyes leaving mine and studying the ground we stood on. "I... we... I can't, Nik. I can't." With a blinding flash of light she was gone and all I was left with was the smoldering remains of the scrubs she had been wearing.

Interlude 1

Double Romantic

Summer 2025, Casita de Soledad, Central Arizona

LICIA CLEARED HER THROAT BEHIND ME. SHE HAD developed quite a habit of reading over my shoulder while I wrote.

I spun around in my chair, covering my irritation with a smile, "Yes, dear?"

"I don't remember it like that," she said, her face serious.

"What?" I asked.

"That speech. First all romantic and then all practical and then double romantic. I don't remember it being that... that... that polished, that sweet, that..." she trailed off as she came over and sat in my lap, kissing me soundly.

I kissed her back, giving as good as I got. "What do you remember me saying?"

She shrugged, her index finger tracing my eyebrow and then my lower lip. "I don't remember the exact words, but you couldn't have been that polished or else how could I have resisted?"

"I don't know how you resisted in the first place," I told her, pulling her close. Our bodies did their thing, exchanging neutronic and electrical energy, the thrill of it undiminished by the years. "What was going on for you that day?"

She sighed and leaned back, looking in my eyes. "I was afraid. Your arguments, while I don't remember them being quite that eloquent, just made it harder."

"Cause you had the hots for me," I offered. She nodded. "And it took everything you had just to keep your hands off of me." I tickled her ribs and she laughed and pushed my hand away.

"Yes, something like that."

"What were you afraid of?" I asked.

She shrugged again. "What we're all afraid of: the end that comes whenever there is a beginning. I eventually told you about my previous relationship, but the pain of it was still too near for me to trust you."

I nodded slowly. She had been hurt deeply by the man that came before me. They had spent five years together, and the end had come suddenly and dramatically about six months before we met and after her transformation to Lightningirl. I had had a similar experience with Ashely Long, but further in the past.

"So should I change it? You know, make it less elegant, more fumbling, not as romantic?"

"No... God no," she said with a smile. "What you can do is say those words to me with the same passion you did on that day. Tell me the romantic part and the practical and then the double romantic part. Say the words like they're brand new." She stood up and backed away a few paces until our bodies stopped interacting. "I'll see if I can resist you again."

"And to think they call me the romantic one."

"Well, just because I'm not 'romantic' doesn't mean that

I don't like a little romance now and then." She stood there staring at me, waiting for me to start, daring me to go all goopy romantic on her.

I took a deep breath. I glanced at the words I had written and then turned away. I didn't want to say the same thing, just be in the same space and see what happened. I looked at her in her khaki shorts and black tank top. Petite with long black hair and lovely curves. Beautiful doesn't go half far enough in describing her. To me she is the most beautiful thing in the world, the reason I get up each day, the reason I draw breath.

She smiled playfully as I stood up and rubbed my sweating palms on my shorts. I took a step forward, but she backed up, keeping out of the reach of our neutrino/electrical reaction.

I stopped and tried to gather my thoughts again. I was out of practice. We weren't in the early phase of the relationship when big words could make a difference. We had been together for two decades and often a look or a hug was more than enough.

But she had asked and it was a reasonable thing to ask for, so I finally opened my mouth and started talking.

"You know all those romantic clichés, the ones in the sappy romantic comedies, that I love and you tolerate?" She nodded. "Well, for me and you, they are literally true. You do complete me, not just emotionally, but in every way—our powers together are so much more than they are apart." She smiled slyly and took a step forward as thin tendrils of energy started to jump between our bodies. "I am a better man with you, so much more than I could have been without you. You are, quite literally, the only one for me. Who else could handle my radioactive personality?" She nodded, moving closer, encouraging me to continue. "Together we changed the world, apart, I shudder to think what would have happened. I can't live without you. I would have been dead many, many times if you hadn't been—"

Her body collided with mine, cutting me off. "Enough," she whispered as she held me tightly.

"See, you can't resist me."

I felt her head, which was buried in my chest, shake as she said, "No I can't. I never really could."

Chapter 19

Friends

Late Winter 2005, Luke Air Force Base, Arizona

I SPENT THE NEXT SEVERAL DAYS WITH SARAH AS SHE recovered. I took it on myself to be her personal bodyguard. To say I didn't trust the military would have been only a slight exaggeration. Even though General Marcus had finally relented, I was left with a bad taste in my mouth.

So I slept in a chair and had my meals brought to me. I helped her to the bathroom and made sure she ate. I tried to engage her in conversation, but she wasn't talkative. I suspect she didn't want to reveal too much about her society, things that we might use to our advantage, and I was the same. We both knew we were being watched. So, I introduced her to the pleasures of daytime TV.

Soap operas, game shows, travel shows, and cooking shows. Surprisingly, she loved them. And it gave us something to do, something to focus on, and something we could talk about.

It was entirely mundane and boring. I think we both loved it. And it was a big deal, spending three days with a humanoid born on another planet, talking about food and travel and the fallibility of humanoid emotions.

I say "humanoid" because she could relate to the soap operas, to what those people were going through, even though they're so melodramatic. This comforted me. Not only did these aliens look like us, they felt like us too.

When it was time, I went with her. She was dressed in jeans and a button-down white shirt. She had taken a shower and looked just like one of us (albeit rather tall with fine blond hair and big teeth). Colonel Williams had given her some ID, a credit card, a cell phone, and some cash.

We got into a jeep that took us to the front gate of Luke Air Force Base.

"Thank you," I told her as we rode towards the gate.

"My thanks go to you," she said with a gentle smile. "My life is owed to you. I will be true. I will speak. What happens, I know not. I am nobody, but I will speak."

"Thank you, Sarah. I hope that they will listen, that we can end this fighting."

"I hope that too."

When we arrived at the gate, I walked her to the waiting cab on the other side. She looked at the cab nervously and then back to me.

"It's okay," I said. "They have promised not to follow."

She nodded and swallowed. "I fear," she said quietly.

"I do too," I told her. We stood there in awkward silence for what seemed like minutes. "Can I hug you good-bye?" I asked.

"What is that?" she asked.

"We saw it on TV. When friends leave each other they often embrace." I pantomimed with my arms showing her what I meant. She nodded and I gently put my arms around her.

"Friends," she whispered in my ear.

She pulled away and got in the cab. As it drove off I felt so much. I felt hopeful and scared, worried and grateful, and very, very confused. Some of the aliens, the ones like Sarah, were so much like us. Why were we fighting? Why did they want to kill us? Could Sarah "speak" and help us?

I didn't get long to think about it. The private who had driven us ran up to me. "You've been summoned back to Palo Verde, sir. It is urgent. A helicopter is waiting."

COLONEL WILLIAMS GREETED ME WITH A SHARP NOD WHEN I climbed into the helicopter. It was just the two of us and we had a few minutes to talk.

"Some things need to change," I told him.

He looked puzzled, his green eyes searching mine, and asked, "Like what?"

"I don't want to be in the dark anymore. I want to know what is going on. I want to be a participant, not just a tool."

Williams sighed, his erect posture deflating somewhat. "Can I be honest with you, Nik?" he asked. I nodded in answer. "I agree, but I'm a soldier and I follow orders."

He didn't tell me what I wanted to hear, but his honesty was refreshing. I smiled and said, "Well I guess I'll have to convince the right people to give the right orders." My smile widened as I envisioned myself flying into the Oval Office and having a heart to heart with the president. "So why are we headed back to Palo Verde?"

"Intelligence has heard some chatter about a terrorist attack. It's unverified, but we want you on site in case anything happens."

"A terrorist attack on Palo Verde?" I asked.

Williams nodded gravely in answer. I couldn't help but

remember what Tom Tyree said: *We anticipate one more attempt on your life in the near future. One from these embedded aliens.*

Chapter 20

Protocol X

Late Winter 2005, Palo Verde Nuclear Generating Station, Arizona

I WAS COOPED UP AT PALO VERDE BECAUSE OF THIS "chatter." It was nice to get fully charged in the reactor, to get some rest, to spend some time with my friend Jennifer Johnson. She was the scientist usually assigned to me and my best friend on the team. But, I quickly got bored. Colonel Williams was kind enough to ask me to stay, although we all knew that it was an order.

Serious training was not done at Palo Verde. Area 51 was the place for that, where there's room and I can't hurt anything. Training a controlled nuclear reaction on the site of the country's largest nuclear reactor is not a good idea. So I worked out, jogged endlessly around the grounds, played video games, and slept.

At least no one was asking me to even pretend to be a janitor anymore. I guess saving the world will do that for you.

On the third day things got exciting, very exciting. I was in the control room, that big cement building that was Neutrinoman central, chatting with Jennifer. We were talking about Licia.

"You know," she said, pushing her black-rimmed glasses up onto her nose, "I think she just needs a little more time. Don't give up."

"Not a chance," I said with a smile. "She's going to have a hell of a time getting rid of me. Did I tell you—"

Jennifer's brown eyes got wide and she pressed her left hand to her ear and the headset that sat there. Her mouth opened and she blinked rapidly. Her eyes locked with mine and I saw fear—no, terror. "There is an incoming missile headed directly for us. Protocol X has been invoked." She spoke quickly.

I hesitated. I wasn't supposed to, that wasn't what Protocol X was about. It was the highest level of emergency and my "orders" were to transform into Neutrinoman immediately and address the threat. But, I was standing a foot away from Jennifer. If I transformed and took off from here, I would kill her. I was in the Neutrinoman control room with half a dozen other people. If I flew straight up from here the fallout from my transformation and crashing through the roof would injure or kill many of them.

When Colonel Williams had briefed me on the protocol, I had suggested we call it "Smash." As in "Neutrinoman Smash!" My pop culture reference to the Incredible Hulk fell flat. It seemed these military types didn't pay much attention to the comics. And frankly, with what had happened since those cosmic rays hit the planet, it seems they should get a crash course or something. Fiction has been preparing us for superheroes for the last eighty years or more.

"The missile is inbound from the south," Jennifer said, her voice cracking. "Go!" she shouted. "Now!"

I turned and started running. I don't care what my orders are, I don't kill my friends. I couldn't do it. I know, I know, I was risking a nuclear disaster to save my friend's life. Well, to tell you the truth I would do the same for a stranger. I'm not Superman, my powers don't manifest benignly. I can't fly without producing dire consequences for biological life in the vicinity.

Once my long strides had carried me a dozen feet from Jennifer I started the transformation. No emptying of pockets, no worrying about replacing my clothes. I was headed for the east entrance, but there was a technician standing there staring. "Move!" I shouted, but he didn't or couldn't, so I veered to the right of him and hit the wall at full speed, fully transformed.

This building is brick and cement. It's no stick-built house. I hit it hard, juicing up my nuclear reaction at the last moment so that I wouldn't just bounce off with an imprint of my body on the wall like some Looney Tunes cartoon character. I went through, but it sucked all my momentum and I ended up in a tangle on the other side of the wall, half buried under bricks and debris. I was a bit disoriented from the impact, but got to my feet and looked to the sky.

To the south I could see a small light moving towards us with the hint of a contrail behind it. I got my bearings and took off, flying hard and fast.

For many miles south of Palo Verde, there is nothing but desert. You have to go about forty miles before you run into the small agricultural town of Gila Bend—the Gila River winds through the desert and makes a ninety-degree turn there, thus the name. There is nothing out there but sand and cactus and rattlesnakes. How had a missile been launched from there? Was it the aliens? Could it really be anyone else? Tom Tyree had warned me another attack was coming and that attack would be directed at me. Blowing up Palo Verde with me in it would not only kill me (theoretically), but it would put much of the country in crisis dealing with the nuclear fallout.

But what about Sarah? It had been three days since she was released. What about her "speaking" on our behalf? Was all her talk just talk, just a way to get away?

I didn't have long to ponder this because the missile soon came into view. It was not the little surface-to-air missile that I had dealt with a few months ago, this thing was big. It was about four feet in diameter and about fifteen feet tall. It had this rough, homemade look to it.

As I approached, I saw a flash of movement on the cone of the missile as a purple energy ball erupted from it.

If there had been any doubt that this was alien sent, that this missile was about me, that doubt evaporated as the scintillating ball of energy shot forward. I dove down trying to avoid the energy ball, but it was too fast. It grazed my left leg, and that jet went out and I went tumbling.

My left leg hurt, like it was on fire, and was quite useless for flying. I stopped the jet on my right leg and used just my arms to stabilize my flight and turn around. When I did, the missile was long past me and headed towards Palo Verde.

I brought my legs together and using my right one for thrust, again headed towards the missile. I wasn't going fast enough. I wasn't going to make it.

I then flashed on the memory of Licia and how she had to climb on my back when I flew us to the hostage standoff with Toxicwasteman. She wanted to stand on my feet, and I told her I couldn't because I needed my hands to fly. She asked why it had to be my hands and legs the neutrino jets came out of to make me fly. Back then we didn't have time to experiment. Now, with the missile getting away, I had no choice.

I stopped the jet from my right leg and pulled my legs up. I then visualized a large yellow jet coming out of my posterior.

Yes, ladies and gentlemen, this is where the infamous Neutrinoman butt-thruster was invented. You've seen the pictures. You've laughed at them, I know you have. But necessity was the mother of this invention.

And it worked, boy did it work. The thrust was a little erratic at first, but the more I focused, and the more I practiced the better I got. I was quickly gaining on the missile, looking like something of a missile myself with a tail of neutronic flame five feet long shooting out of my ass. Who said saving lives has to look dignified.

I used my hands to steady and maneuver myself and was soon coming up on the missile. I hadn't come up with a plan, being so preoccupied with this new thrusting technique, and with Palo Verde now clearly in sight, I didn't have but seconds to act. My first thought was to just run into the warhead from the side (where it couldn't shoot at me again) and take it out. But what if it was nuclear? Having a missile and a superhero explode at this altitude would not be a good idea. An alternate plan took shape in my head and I acted.

I thrust hard, letting my reaction grow very hot and collided with the tail end of the missile. I did this from above hoping to do two things: sheer off its fins so it couldn't maneuver anymore; and push the nose upward so that it would miss Palo Verde.

I hit the top portion of the bottom of the missile hard, my yellow neutronic reaction melting through the tail fin, the missile casing, and the nozzle. I was awash in yellow flames and couldn't see a thing.

What do you know about missile design? I really don't know much but what I learned as a kid launching Estes rockets into the sky. The engine is pretty simple. You have a bunch of fuel, a chamber for that fuel to react in, and a nozzle for the gasses of the reaction to escape from. The nozzle is crucial. It lets the gasses out in a single direction in a controlled fashion to create thrust (just like what I was doing with my posterior right then).

What happens when you take the nozzle away from a rocket? Well, you might think it would explode, but it doesn't. Sorry. If you block the nozzle and all that pressure doesn't have anywhere to go, then it will explode. But with no nozzle, the gasses will escape in a less focused, less directed way.

Once I was clear of the missile and could see again, I saw that I had taken out two of the fins and the nozzle. The back end of the missile was ragged with fire spewing out of the back end as the missile spun slowly end over end.

As I headed back towards it, I assessed its trajectory. It looked to me like it was still going to land near Palo Verde, and just because I had disabled its propulsion didn't make it any less dangerous.

I flew fast, my butt-thruster beginning to feel more natural, and maneuvered myself so I was under the missile as it spun and fell towards the ground.

I watched it spin, and after the cone was pointed down (and fortunately didn't fire at me again) I moved up so that when the cone came to a horizontal position I was right underneath it. I thrust up, my shoulders hitting the midsection of the missile. I brought my arms up, fists clenched, and buried them into the missile. This left me with just the butt-thruster and my right foot to fly with. I focused first on arresting the spin of the missile and managed that. My head was down and the ground was rapidly approaching. The missile was going to impact short of Palo Verde, but depending on what the payload was, it could still be devastating.

I then used my butt-thruster to arrest the downward momentum of the missile and started pushing it back up into the sky.

What would Superman do with a disabled missile? I remember this in one of the movies. He would fly it up into the atmosphere and with a mighty shove break it free of the gravity well where it would float off harmlessly.

It made sense to me, so I set about doing just that. I flew as fast as I could, watching the Earth retreat below me becoming smaller and smaller. I had done this enough so I knew what to expect, so I didn't freak out as I began to see the curvature of the Earth. I wasn't sure how high I needed to be, but when it felt like my momentum was continuing to carry me away without any thrust, I pulled my arms out of the missile.

I looked at it floating in the black void of space. Inert like that it looked somewhat benign, and in examining it I could clearly see a roughness to it. As if it was homemade or hastily constructed.

The aliens. The Arcturian Alliance. They had created this. They had launched it at Palo Verde, at me. I reversed my thrust, using just my hands, and watched as the missile slowly moved away. I felt sad and angry. Sad that Sarah had either been lying or had been ineffective. It had been three days—if she were "speaking," shouldn't the attacks have stopped? And I was angry at these beings so like us, but still they wanted us dead.

I turned my back on the missile and began thrusting for home. My left leg was coming back so I used the more dignified foot thrusters to push me homeward. It wasn't long until I realized the missile wasn't the only attack on Palo Verde today.

Chapter 21

Arrogance Precedes a Fall
Late Winter 2005, Palo Verde Nuclear Generating Station, Arizona

DISCARDING THE MISSILE TOOK A FEW HOURS. I CAN FLY fast, but it takes a while to get up high enough. As I got close to Palo Verde, I noticed the barest flickering of light at the power plant. Something was very wrong about that. I reengaged by butt-thruster and increased my speed. The tiny flash resolved into little tendrils of blue-white lightning.

Lightningirl was down there and she was throwing bolts of electricity. But why? What was going on?

I was well into the atmosphere now and falling fast, very fast. As the landscape resolved I could see that there were some vehicles at the front gate of Palo Verde, that Lightningirl stood in the grounds, lightning arcing from the power plant behind her, to her, and then to these vehicles. I could also see that the security booth was destroyed, there were some smoldering pits in the ground, and what appeared to be gunfire was emanating from the vehicles toward Lightningirl.

Another attack. This one by ground. Yeah, I was mad, and I was sick and tired of this. I had been pushed and pushed and now I had been pushed too far. The image of that dead alien in Yellowstone flashed in my mind and then an image of Sarah injured and bleeding in her craft. I pushed them down, it was time to get past this squeamishness I had about killing the aliens. It was past time. They were unrelenting in their attacks. They had left me no choice.

I waited until the last possible moment and reversed the direction of my thrust. The last possible moment being about five thousand feet in the air. So it was not like they didn't know I was coming. I was going very fast, so the amount of thrust I had to apply to slow me down was tremendous. As Licia tells it, I was this huge yellow fireball descending from the heavens.

Even with that I landed hard, but my aim was good, so I crash landed between Lightningirl and the aliens. As I stood up in the crater I had created, I couldn't see a thing. There was a thick cloud of dust that my thrusters and impact had kicked up.

"Lightningirl," I called out, I was unsure where she was and where the vehicles were.

"Over here," I heard her call back to me.

A barrage of gunfire erupted after we spoke. They were shooting blindly into the dust trying to hit us. Which was odd—didn't they know it wouldn't do any good?

As I walked to where I thought Lightningirl was, I felt a bullet penetrate my neutrino form. It hit my right shoulder and went right through me coming out the other side without doing any harm. The bullet itself would be a bit melted and slightly radioactive, but no harm came to me. The military had tested this in the early days. I wasn't bullet-proof, but bullets didn't hurt me. I am a controlled nuclear reaction. Is a bullet going to harm the sun?

"What the hell is going on?" I said as I walked towards her.

"Oh, just some overly enthusiastic Neutrinoman group-ies," she said. "You know how they get." At that moment I didn't know how they could get, but with my identity revealed it was coming and soon.

"Really?" I said. "They seem to be here for you, diehard fans of the fairer q-morph." I had to yell to make myself heard over the crackle of the lightning bolt she was drawing from the power plant.

"The missile?" she asked, serious now.

"Gone," I said.

She smiled. I came just close enough that our forms started to interact. It felt good, real good. "You need a charge?" she asked. I nodded and she started directing the energy of Palo Verde into me. It hurt fiercely, but in a good way.

I turned from her to face the aliens. The dust was clear-ing, and I was beginning to make out the vehicles. With Lightningirl feeding me energy, I slowly started walking forward. The bullets had stopped and I could hear some mumbling coming from our attackers.

I could see the smoldering ruins of a military jeep and a security truck on this side of the fence. There wasn't a lot of military personal stationed there then. Security, yes, troops, no. It looked like the aliens had dealt with them pretty easily. I saw five bodies on our side, and only Light-ningirl had kept them at bay.

I studied the vehicles. They were not that impressive. Three pickup trucks and a dump truck. They all looked pretty normal, but as I studied them some differences became apparent. They each had metal welded onto the front of them over the grill. There were plates behind the cab of the pickup trucks that provided cover for the gunmen that stood there pointing their weapons at me.

They all showed evidence of the lightning bolts that had been directed at them. Blackened metal, shattered windshields, prone alien bodies on the ground.

The aliens were all of the tall, blond-haired variety. There were about a dozen of them, both male and female. As I let the dust continue to settle, I thought of what Toxicwasteman had said, about them being resource constrained. From what I saw of the missile and looking at these vehicles, that appeared to be true. Where was the spaceship raining hell on us that we would have had a hard time stopping? They had human weapons. Where were the exotic energy weapons that could take both me and Lightningirl out easily? Why were they shooting lead at us? They must know it wouldn't harm us.

I got close enough to see the looks in their eyes: fear. I stood there, a controlled nuclear reaction with a thick lightning bolt feeding energy into me from the nuclear power plant behind me via the controlled electrical reaction that is Lightningirl. Fear was logical.

"Who is in command here?" I shouted. "Lower your weapons and send your leader out."

I WAS FEELING A BIT COCKY, I WILL ADMIT IT. I COULDN'T see how these aliens with their conventional weapons and ragged vehicles could hurt us. Lightningirl and I were more than enough to hold them off.

They lowered their weapons and there was some whispered conversation that I couldn't quite make out over the crackling of the lightning bolt that was striking my back. But, before long, an alien approached. He was tall and proud with long blond hair pulled back in a ponytail and piercing blue eyes.

"I am in command," he shouted as he approached me. He stood between me and the dump truck. "My name is Kothlan."

His command of the English language was much better than Sarah's. He talked like one of us, with a bit of an accent that seemed vaguely European. He wore jeans and a T-shirt and he was covered in brown dust. He looked like a construction worker, not an alien terrorist.

I glanced back at Lightningirl and held up my hand telling her to stop the energy feed. The snapping and crackling of the electricity made it hard to hold a conversation. "Why do you attack us, Kothlan?" I asked.

"These are my orders," he said. "Your people must die."

"Why?"

He shrugged stiffly, like the gesture wasn't natural to him, but one he had practiced. "The council has decreed it so. That is all I need to know."

It was like talking to Marcus or Williams. They were all just following orders.

"You cannot win here," I said. "Have your soldiers drop their weapons and come forward."

He nodded and turned and shouted to his people. The language he used had harsh guttural sounds with clicks. Underneath his shout I heard a brief metallic groan, which I didn't have time to ponder. His men had held their position.

"I don't want to fight you," I said, increasing the rate of

my reaction as a display of force. And here's the truth, my reticence here was a problem. My not being a soldier was a problem. My hesitation was a problem. And they took advantage of that.

"Very well," Kothlan said as he stepped aside. Several things happened at once. I noticed that the front of the dump truck looked different, where the left headlight had been was now an empty hole. That must have been what happened when I heard the metallic sound. The rest of the aliens had drawn their weapons and were pointing them at me.

And, most importantly, a purple ball of energy shot out of that hole and hit me square in the chest.

My whole body felt strange, numb and tingly at the same time. My neutrino form fled and flesh returned. My knees buckled and I fell to the ground naked. I saw Kothlan grin. This was a trap. I had walked right into it. They were going to kill me.

As consciousness fled and my body fell forward, I heard guns fire and Lightningirl shout "No!"

Interlude 2

Your Turn

Summer 2025, Casita de Soledad, Central Arizona

"IT'S YOUR TURN NOW," I SAID. WE WERE SITTING AT OUR small table in our dining area. We were surrounded by windows facing south, affording us with a nice view of our high desert home. It was dinnertime at Casita de Soledad. Tonight we dined on a salad from the garden and cheese (of course).

She shook her head. "I cooked, you've got KP duty."

"No. It's your turn to write."

She looked up at me, chewing her salad as she studied my face. She swallowed and said, "No it's not. This is your thing, not mine."

She had become supportive of my project, I think she saw the good it was doing me, but had never shown any desire to participate directly. We were at a point in the story that needed to be told, but I couldn't tell it. "We are fighting the aliens in front of Palo Verde. They've forced me back to my human form and are about to kill me. I can't tell this part of the story."

She blinked several times, her brown eyes a little wider

than normal. She put her fork down, stood up, and walked away. A moment later I heard the front door open and close. I sighed, grabbed several pieces of cheese, and followed her.

I FOUND HER UP NEAR THE POWER LINES, NEAR OUR launching pad, on the highest point of our property. She was sitting on a rock facing west watching the sun go down over the rolling hills.

"Can you tell me about it?" I asked as I squatted next to her. "What happened there was a crucial moment for the war... for us."

She nodded, her mouth set in a thin line, her eyes avoiding mine as they searched the horizon.

"It won't be hard. You can just dictate and I'll write it down," I offered.

"Ohh, *that's* going to make it easier," she turned and I saw the tears and the remembered fear in her eyes. "I almost lost you that day, Nik. I have no desire to relive it."

I nodded. "I know it's hard. Too many times we've almost lost each other, we've almost lost everything. I understand. But it helps to write it down. It helps to tell the story."

"No," she said, turning back to the sunset.

I sat next to her and silently watched the sun set over the desert. The dust in the air caught the last light of the day and turned them a beautiful orange/brown. It was a cloudless evening so it wasn't that spectacular, but it was nice.

I knew my girl well enough to know she needed space with this. For the next three days I didn't say a word, but I didn't write either. It seemed silly to continue without her part of the story. And without my writing I was restless. I sat around watching movies or working in the yard.

I was bored and it showed. I was going a bit stir-crazy and couldn't hide it.

In truth, I missed the writing. I needed the writing. And I guess she didn't. She occupied herself with her garden, with cooking, with taking care of the household. A simple life, a fine life, but it just wasn't enough for me. She may not have needed to write, but after three days of living with me not writing, she came to the conclusion that she needed me to write.

"Okay," she said with a sigh. She turned the flat screen off and stood in front of it, her arms crossed. "I'll do it. I can't stand you this way. Since you started writing you've been…"

"A lot more pleasant to be around," I offered.

"Yes," she said with a smile. "I will help you with this one part just to get you writing again. This is your thing, not mine."

"Understood," I said as I grabbed my laptop and sat back down on the couch. She paced back and forth in front of me as she told her part of the story.

Chapter 22

The Battle of Palo Verde
Late Winter 2005, Palo Verde Nuclear Generating Station, Arizona

Nik's note: Licia told this story directly to me, and I have recorded her words verbatim. So when she says "you" she is referring to me.

WHERE DO I START? I GUESS THIS ISN'T AS EASY AS IT looks, trying to patch together memories and emotions into something coherent enough to read.

The Battle of Palo Verde.

On that day I was up at Area 51. It was the preferred training area for us q-morphs. It was big, well guarded, and in the middle of nowhere. High-tension power lines run through the base so I am well powered. I was on the dry lake bed doing some accuracy training. They had run power to part of it, and I was tapping the power and practicing firing at small targets about twenty yards away. Each target was about a foot in diameter and had a colored light in the middle of it. When it turned red I would zap it with a small lightning bolt and it would turn green. They were measuring my reaction time and accuracy, trying to make me better.

Jack Johnson was the scientist on site and there was

a lieutenant, whose name I can't remember, running the show. It was actually kind of fun, and useful. I was slowly getting faster and better with my lightning.

"WAIT," LICIA SAID AS SHE STOPPED PACING AND LOOKED at me, her face serious. "Did you want me to talk about my feelings and emotions like you do? How my every thought was of us being apart, how I couldn't live without you, how..." her little tirade ended in laughter. Like I said, she's not the most romantic person in the world.

I kept my cool and said, "That would be nice. Maybe you can give us a little more context. After all, this is a love story I am writing."

She nodded her head, restarted her pacing, and continued her story.

I GUESS IF I AM BEING HONEST, YOU WERE ON MY MIND. A lot, actually. I mean, I am not the most romantic person and don't consider myself to be driven by that kind of passion. But... I mean... Well, that speech you gave at Luke had an impact. I had never been involved with a man that talked like that about me. That felt that intensely about me.

God this is hard. Do I really have to do this?

Okay. You asked for it.

What I was feeling was confused. I cared for you and I thought that I could love you, but in truth I was not in love with you yet. I was on the edge of that cliff looking over, yes, but I had not "fallen." And that damn romantically practical speech was on my mind. I knew we had to be a team. I understood that the way we worked together, the way our q-morph forms interacted, was decidedly intimate. But I wasn't ready for more. Being Lightningirl was really plenty for me to cope with at that point. I didn't want to add a romantic relationship on top of it.

And I had some of the same worries as you did since the accident. Namely, would I ever find a lover that could handle the transformed me? One that could handle who I had become. What if passion got too passionate and I hurt my lover? You had the same problem. And I had to admit I was curious what a physical relationship would be like between us. What was clear is that both of us could handle the other's power and that if it got physical, it would be... well, you know how that turned out.

So there's some emotional stuff for you... Anyway, where was I?

It was early afternoon when Jack came running over, a serious look on his face. Jack is Jennifer Johnson's husband, and they are two of the scientists that worked with you and me a lot back then. He said, "You are needed at Palo Verde. Now. Protocol X has been invoked."

I remember when Colonel Williams briefed us on Protocol X—dumb name, by the way. It was this serious presentation complete with PowerPoint slides. Protocol Alpha: life as normal, at ease soldier. Protocol Gama: be on alert (our usual status, I don't actually recall them ever invoking Alpha while the war was going on. Protocol Zebra: engage the enemy, protect the innocent. And Protocol X: execute your orders ASAP without regard to collateral damage.

It reminded me of the defcon levels from the Cold War. I understand the need for short-handing this kind of thing, but it seemed a little coarse for my taste.

"What's happening?" I asked him. Jack's a good man and he looked scared. It's not a look I had ever seen on his handsome face. Protocol X is kind of the "blame the messenger" protocol. If the person delivering the message is close to you, they might be harmed by the quickness of your action. I've always thought that was crap. I was backing away from him as we spoke. I didn't need a lot of distance to avoid electrocuting him when I went elemental, but I needed some.

"Palo Verde is under attack. A missile is headed for it and Neutrinoman has gone after it. They want you on site just in case." Jack was smart enough to be backing up too.

"Well, that is urgent," I said. I ran a few more steps away from him and then went fully elemental, my electric form jumping onto the power line that snaked from the high-tension power lines to the dry lake bed.

I guess you want me to talk about the experience of being fully elemental?

Well, it's primal. The state reminds me a bit of rock climbing, like at the end of a long ascent when my body is tired enough that my brain shuts up. It is just the rock and me. No past, no future, just one hold at a time, up the cliff, slow and steady. Being elemental is like that. My normal mind isn't there. There is intent (traveling to Palo Verde in this case) and little else.

I know the power grids well. Early on after the accident I studied them. I know where all the high-tension power lines are. I know it deep enough that when I am elemental, when my waking mind is mostly shut down, I still know where I am going.

It is, though, very important to hold my destination firmly in mind before going fully elemental. If you don't, you will end up at the oddest places.

So a few seconds later I was standing, in my humanoid

q-morph form, in the midst of the nest of transformers and towers behind Palo Verde.

Jennifer Johnson was just outside the transformers waiting with a robe. She looked a bit pale, and given her African-American heritage, that is saying something.

"You okay, Jen?" I asked.

She nodded as I let go of my q-morph form and returned to biological, putting on the robe she provided. "Just... I was with Nik when the call came in." She pointed to the headset she was wearing. "Protocol X and I was right next to him."

I smiled, relieved that she was okay, that you hadn't done anything silly, and that I had gotten far enough away from her husband before I transformed.

She filled me in as we walked to the control room. But it was all "hurry up and wait." You had intercepted the missile and when I got to the control room everyone was huddled around the monitors watching you. I hadn't known they had such good cameras at Palo Verde, but they did. At first you were a far off speck and then it was quite up close and personal.

There was a collective gasp when the missile fired its energy weapon at you. We could see the effect it had on your leg. Then there was collective giggle when you first used your—what do you call it?—your butt-thruster. For my own part, I was a bit angry. I know now that you were improvising in the moment, but it made me wonder if you had been putting me on when you made me climb on your back after we got called to take care of Toxicwasteman.

The missile, as we now know, had a dual purpose. They hoped it would work, that it would destroy Palo Verde and you, but failing that they wanted it to distract us. And watching you deal with a missile with an unknown payload was certainly a distraction.

We watched as you carried it into orbit. They had some satellites up there, even then, that could keep an eye on you. They then tapped into a NASA feed that was tracking the missile moving away from Earth and your return.

We were riveted.

Which is why we didn't notice the trucks approaching the front gate until they started firing on the guardhouse. A panicked call came in over the radio. I didn't hear the first part of it, until one of the security team turned up the volume. "...weapons. We need backup! This doesn't look—" there was the sound of automatic weapons fire and the voice stopped. I recognized the voice. His name was Ben and I remember his smile the most—he always had one for me when I drove in.

I ran as fast as I could. I heard some feet behind me, the four soldiers that were in the control room, but I paid them no heed. As soon as I got out of the control room, I transformed into Lightningirl. I hadn't realized it until that day, but I can run a lot faster in my q-morph form. I was like some damn Olympic sprinter as I made my way to the guard station.

As I ran I heard the sound of automatic weapons and an explosion. I drove myself to run faster. I kept thinking of Ben. When I arrived, the scene was chaos.

Interlude 3

Ben

Summer 2025, Casita de Soledad, Central Arizona

LICIA'S PACING ENDED AS SHE FACED AWAY FROM ME, looking west out the living room window.

"Honey?" I asked.

"Ben," she said.

"I'm sorry," I said.

"It's not like we were really friends," Licia said. "It's just that... I knew him. He was a nice man with three kids and a wife of twenty years. He was about forty with brown hair and blue eyes. He liked to garden, was into growing heirloom tomatoes. He gifted me with a few of them once. He was a nice man and..."

I sighed and felt bad I was putting her through this. We, for some years, had been living a life where we both ignored the past. We did this by living our simple little existence at Casita de Soledad (lonely little house). The government contributed by happily hiding us away out here, but wanting to keep us around "just in case." And for the large part, the world did too. The world wanted to move on, move past those tumultuous years. And here I was dredging it all up.

Writing it all down. I felt bad about it, but like many, many things in my life since I became Neutrinoman, I may have felt bad about it, but I knew it was the right thing.

I put my laptop down, got up, and pulled her into a hug. "He was the first," she said as she silently cried. "He was the first person I knew to die in this war."

"But not the last," I offered.

"No, not the last," she agreed.

Chapter 23

Going Elemental

Late Winter 2005, Palo Verde Nuclear Generating Station, Arizona

Nik's Note: More from Licia.

THIS WAS BEFORE PALO VERDE WAS COMPLETELY TAKEN over by the military. The troops stationed there were minimal. When I arrived, the scene was already chaos. An overturned jeep burning; three bodies on the ground, one of them Ben's; the gatehouse on fire; the four vehicles with the aliens in the back; and three soldiers trying to hold the aliens off.

Something struck me as odd about the scene. Well, several things, actually. Why hadn't the dump truck crashed through the gate? It could have easily. What did they want? What were they even doing here? The front gate didn't matter, if they were trying to do real mischief they would have crashed through the gate and run a car bomb, or something, into the reactor. Before Palo Verde was reinforced, this wouldn't have been that hard to do.

All of that went through my mind, bothered me, but I didn't have much time to think about it. Ben was there lying in the middle of it all, still and unmoving. He must have come out of the guardhouse to confront the aliens.

I leapt into the fray shooting lightning bolts at the blond-headed aliens. They stopped firing at the soldiers and fired at me. I never liked that sensation—bullets passing through my lightning form—but it wasn't harmful, not in the least.

The aliens, they looked almost normal. They were dressed in jeans and flannel shirts. But, oddly, they also had on huge rubber gloves and these big black boots.

I extended my left hand back towards Palo Verde and started tapping into its power, a large bolt of lightning arching from the closest power line to my hand.

I had to again wonder what this was all about. Judging from past behavior, the aliens were smart. Shooting at me wasn't smart, especially when I was so well powered. If this was truly an attack, not advancing past the gate was plain stupid.

I took a few of them down with my lightning, or at least I thought I had. They disappeared from view into the back of the dump truck or pickup trucks.

I held my position, trying to defend the soldiers, prevent more casualties. I regret that. I should have taken the battle to them. I should have been more aggressive. But after seeing Ben, it was all I could do.

This lasted for a while. Them shooting. Me firing lightning bolts. I was, frankly, getting bored with it and was about to move in when you showed up.

Your entrance was... it was... well, let's just say it was dramatic and hilarious at the same time. At first I couldn't see much, just a yellow fireball heading towards us. If not for that distinctive color I might have thought it was an alien weapon of some sort. And then I got to see your butt-thruster live and in person. I almost laughed. Sorry, hon, but really, shouldn't I have laughed?

You slammed down and the dust from your impact stopped the battle. When the dust cleared you had your little conversation with Kothlan, the alien leader, and they fired their hidden weapon at you.

It all made sense then. This seemingly inept plan of attack of theirs was not about attacking Palo Verde, it was about killing you.

You went down as that huge purple ball of energy slammed into you. First you went to your knees and then to the ground, a devilish grin of victory on Kothlan's face.

They all pointed their guns at you. They were going to execute you.

I shouted, "No!" and... well, it is a little fuzzy here, even for me. I went elemental. There was no time. I couldn't let them kill you. I had to save you.

The aliens had prepared for me. The back of the dump truck and the pickup trucks were lined with rubber. They had thick soled shoes and rubber gloves on. They were expecting lightning and they had done their best to insulate against it.

But they were not prepared for the elemental me.

As you went down, as I shouted "no," I reached back and tapped even more power from Palo Verde, a lightning bolt the size of a tree trunk arcing from the nearest high-tension power lines to my left hand. My need for speed was so intense, my need to save you so all-encompassing, that I became that Palo Verde fed lightning bolt. We were one.

We call this going "elemental" for a reason. Well, more for the lack of "reason." My consciousness faded into this primal need. To save you. Until that moment I hadn't known what I could truly do.

I became lightning and the lightning that I was stabbed out, striking each of the rifle-wielding aliens. They were insulated, yes, but not enough, and they had no protection from the plasma.

One hundred million volts, thirty thousand degrees Kelvin, much hotter than the surface of the sun. They didn't have a chance. This wasn't the delicate tendrils of electricity that I had been firing at them. This was everything Palo Verde and I had striking them. One by one they went down until only Kothlan was left and I found myself back in my Lightningirl form standing over you right in front of him.

He had drawn a handgun and was pointing it at you.

"Put the gun down," I said.

He looked at me, his icy blue eyes boring into me. "We will not fail," he said.

I couldn't stop the bullet so I stopped him the only way I could. I hit him with the full force available to me and he went flying back and crashed into the front of the dump truck. His body fell and landed on the ground, unmoving.

Interlude 4

Signs of Being Human
Summer 2025, Casita de Soledad, Central Arizona

I LOOKED AT LICIA AND SMILED, BUT SHE DIDN'T NOTICE. Those early days were hard. Each death that we witnessed was hard. The ones that we caused all the more so.

"I was thinking," I began, "we should get a papaya tree into the greenhouse. You know, a dwarf variety like the banana tree. I know you could make it grow." Her eyes met mine as she blinked back the memories and took a slow deep breath.

She nodded. "That's a good idea. I love papayas." She slowly rose, rubbing her palms on her shorts. "I'll go see if there is a good spot."

I let her go. We didn't discuss that battle again. I know telling her part of the story was hard on her, but it was an important turning point in what would come. Those early encounters with the aliens changed us, made us confront the reality of this war, forced us to grow in our powers and to grow up.

This life we've led has been amazing. An unparalleled adventure, but also filled with unparalleled difficulties. With great power comes a great burden: the weight of responsibility. During those years I often found myself feeling jealous of Toxicwasteman. He didn't seem to be burdened by his power or feel guilt over his actions. He waged his own war with the aliens laughing all the way.

But then again, he was psychotic. So the burden and guilt Licia and I felt were difficult but signs that we were human.

Chapter 24

Get Me Out of Here

Late Winter 2005, Palo Verde Nuclear Generating Station, Arizona

Nik's Note: Licia is done and we're back to me telling the story.

SEARING PAIN WAS MY BEACON BACK TO CONSCIOUSNESS. It felt like an elephant was standing on my chest, one with spiked heels on, one that liked to tap dance.

I could hear the roaring crackle of electricity and smell the sharp tang of ozone. My body relaxed around it before I really knew what was going on and the pain subsided to a bearable level.

"What?" I mumbled as my eyes fluttered open.

I took a deep breath. "Wake up," I heard a feminine voice say. The voice was frayed at the edges, urgent.

That urgency brought me back faster, I focused and I could see Lightningirl standing over me. I was lying in the dirt. I could also smell burned metal, charred flesh, and urine. I shook my head trying to clear it and looked around.

I was on the dirt where I had fallen in front of the dump truck. Kothlan's body was there limp and lifeless, the source of the charred flesh and urine smell. I turned away and saw Lightningirl. She was standing over me, her eyes too wide.

I saw some jeeps approaching with military personnel and could hear sirens in the distance.

"Can you handle more?" she asked.

I nodded, struggling to my feet, wondering what the hurry was, if there was another attack coming. The bolt hit me square in the chest and I stumbled back until I was pressed against the dump truck, right where their energy weapon had fired. I took the electricity and used it to change to my neutrino form. I could handle the energy better then and sighed in relief.

The soldiers and scientists were keeping their distance. Looking at Lightningirl, it was no wonder. She was upset, and something was driving her, but I couldn't tell what.

Williams was shouting at us, but I couldn't make him out over the crackling of the lightning. Lightningirl walked up to me, still firing the bolt into me, until we were standing only inches apart.

"Can you fly?" she shouted.

She was pouring the energy into me and I was coming back to myself. I nodded. She grabbed me, pulling me closer and stepping on my feet. The electricity from Palo Verde was still pouring into her and into me. "Get me out of here," she shouted into my ear.

I looked around, no one was close, only the corpse of Kothlan. I didn't know exactly what was going on with her, but I knew she needed me. And that was, really, all I needed to know.

I took off slowly and was glad to see people step back even farther. The electricity from Palo Verde continuing to pump into us until we were several hundred yards high.

"Where do you want to go?" I asked her once we were up about 1,000 feet.

"I don't care," she whispered, holding me much tighter than she needed to. "Just take me away."

I took one last look at the scene below. Police and fire had arrived. There were people all over the place examining the bodies of the aliens lying prone on the ground or in the back of their vehicles. I saw Ben, the other guards, and the soldiers. I flashed back to Yellowstone and the first alien that I had killed.

I held her tight and carefully flew us north.

I WAS GLAD TO GET THE EARTH BACK UNDER MY FEET. I had flown us to that area in Central Arizona between Phoenix and the Verde Valley. Beautiful high desert, rolling hills, deep canyons. It was isolated, and the last time we had been here she had told me we couldn't be together.

I felt that parting, that pain as we stood there. She was still holding me. I had picked this spot because, at this point, I knew it well, because it was isolated, and because it was right next to high-tension power lines.

"Do you want to talk about it?" I asked.

I could feel her head shake in answer. She wasn't okay, and I had complete empathy for what she was feeling. This wasn't the movies—it's not an easy thing to take a life, even the life of an enemy. Especially not the first time.

I took my neutrino reaction down to a minimum and found her doing the same with her electrical reaction. I pushed away so I could see her face. What I saw shocked me.

Her face was hard and sad, but there was such a need

there, such an intense need I didn't know what to do. I doubted that I could ever meet a need that strong.

She stepped back until our bodies stopped interacting and let go of her q-morph form. "Do you want me?" she asked. She stood there naked, looking beautiful and vulnerable and cold.

Did I want her? Was there a more unnecessary question ever asked in the history of mankind? Of course I wanted her. I was desperate to hold her, to touch her. I would have been happy to have ignored the cold and the rocks, to let go of my neutrino form go and make love to her right then and there.

But I didn't.

"I do," I said slowly. "But not like this. Not when you're..."

Tears rolled down her cheeks as she slowly nodded. She wiped them off, sniffed, and then her face hardened again. "You're a good man, Nik," she said. And then with a crack and a flash she was gone. I saw her flash of energy going north.

I stood there in shock for a few minutes before flying back to Palo Verde alone.

Chapter 25

Let's Be a Mess Together
Late Winter 2005, Flagstaff, Arizona

I CHECKED MY PHONE, THE CELL RECEPTION WAS GOOD. I looked down at the dirt trail, remnants of snow and mud from the last snow storm still present. The scenery was stunning. Mount Elden sat large not far away to the north and the east. The San Francisco Peaks loomed to the north, two tall peaks covered in snow. I was walking the trails of Buffalo Park which sat high on a mesa on the north end of Flagstaff.

The air was crisp and cool and a group of clouds were stuck on the Peaks.

"Hi," I said. The phone had rung for a long time before she picked up. It had been five days since the Battle of Palo Verde.

"Hi," she answered.

"Williams said that you are out, no more Lightningirl for you. Is that true?" I asked. Maybe not the most graceful way to get the conversation rolling, but I wasn't about to ask her how she was doing. I knew she wasn't doing well.

"Yeah," she said. "I can't do this 'saving the world' thing, Nik. I'm just not wired for it."

"I understand," I said.

"Thanks." An awkward silence filled up the space between us. I was beginning to think the call had dropped when she said, "Listen, Nik. About the other day, I—"

"It's okay," I said.

"I just wanted to thank you for being such a gentleman. I was in a bad place."

"Yeah," I said, that damn silence filling up the space between us again. I had something to say, but the fear I felt was holding me back. This was the kind of moment you only really get one chance at.

"Well... I... I should probably be going," she said quietly.

I took a deep breath and pushed back the doubts babbling in my head. I kicked at the dirt trail and looked at the craggy face of Mount Elden, ponderosa pine trees sticking up from its steep slope, snow still on the ground. I had something to say and I knew I would regret it for the rest of my life if I didn't get it out.

"Look," I began, "I don't care if you are Lightningirl or not, if you ever use your powers again or not. I don't care about that. What I care about is *you*. What I want is to be with you. I know what you are going through is so hard. I am, and have been, going through the same thing. I..." I trailed off, losing my nerve. I wanted to bare my soul, my pain, all of it. I wanted to give her everything, but it was so hard. Speaking things like this, drawing difficult emotions up, is healthy, but painful.

"Go on," she said so quietly I almost didn't hear it.

"I see that alien, that first one from Yellowstone, whenever I close my eyes. I see that gaping hole in his chest that my neutrino bolt made. I see the unnatural way his limbs rest on the ground. I see his open eyes and the blue of his irises. I smell his charred flesh. I don't seem to be able to get that smell out of my nose.

"I understand, Licia. I understand what you are going through. I am going through it too. If anyone in this world understands what you are experiencing, I do. And you know what? I don't care. Wait... Sorry..." I was scrambling, afraid I had blown it. "I *do* care that you are hurting, I do. But, it is not relevant to what I want."

"And what do you want?" she asked.

I was surprised that she had to ask. But, maybe she wanted to hear it again. "You know how I feel about you. But let me make it absolutely clear. I am crazy about you. I can't stop thinking about you. You are the most beautiful woman I have ever met. I love you." I took a deep breath and said, "Licia Lopez, will you be my girlfriend?"

After I said it, I panicked. I wanted to throw the phone down and run away. "Be my girlfriend," what the hell was I thinking? Were we in third grade or something?

I listened closely, not wanting to miss a thing. I heard the rustle of clothing and then a sniff. I heard a slow shuddering intake of breath. "Yes," she said with a sniff. She was crying. "Yes, Nik Nichols, I will be your girlfriend."

Tears were running down my cheeks. "Oh, thank God," I blurted.

I heard her sniff and laugh. "But I'm such a mess, you know," she said.

"Me too," I said. "Let's be a mess together."

"Okay, how soon can you get here?" she asked.

"Where is here?" I asked.

"I'm at home, in Flag. At my new place, it's south of town just a bit. I can text you the address."

"Well," I said with a smile, "I can be there in about ten minutes then."

"Ten?" she asked. "It might be better if you drive and not fly in as Neutrinoman. That could cause some attention."

"No, Licia. I'm in Flagstaff. I can drive to where you are in ten minutes or so. Flag is not that big."

"What? Wait... you... you planned this?" she sputtered.

"No, no, it wasn't like that," I said, talking quickly. "I finally got clear of Palo Verde and started driving. I was thinking of you and it wasn't until I was here that I got up the nerve to call. I didn't—"

Her laughter cut off my little scramble. "It's okay, Nik," she said. "It's okay if you planned it. Or if you didn't."

"Oh," was all I could say. I still didn't have a bead on her sense of humor. "Good."

"I just texted you my address. Give me an hour, though. I'm a mess. I need a shower and some time to get myself together."

I spent the next forty-five minutes walking the trails of Buffalo Park. It was a long forty-five minutes.

Interlude 5

Be My Girlfriend
Summer 2025, Casita de Soledad, Central Arizona

"'BE MY GIRLFRIEND,'" LICIA SAID WITH A CHUCKLE. "YOU were so cute."

"Hey!" I said, getting up from my lounge chair in the sun and pulling the papers away from her where she sat on the patio. "If you're going to make fun, you don't have to read."

She pulled the papers back. "I'm not making fun, and you were so cute."

I flopped back down on the lounge chair with a sigh.

"You know," she began, "I don't understand the heterosexual male's distaste for the word 'cute.' What's wrong with it?"

"Puppies are cute," I said.

"And girls love puppies. They want to touch them and hold them and kiss them. What's wrong with that?"

I gave her the "you already know the answer to that" look.

"Oh," she said. "It's about sex, isn't it?"

I nodded.

"You want the girl to say you are handsome or strong

or virile. A mighty stud. Right? You want the compliment to be one step away from getting in bed?"

"Something like that," I said.

Her laughter rang out over the high desert. It was clear and bright. And while I was glad she was having a good laugh, I wasn't happy that it was at my expense. "I'm sorry," she began, "let me rephrase. 'Be my girlfriend,' that's such a studly thing to say, so hot, so virile, so... so..." she dissolved back into laughter.

I sighed and stared at her. She was digging in hard, and I had enough perspective to let her. What I had written, what I had dictated from her, what she had just read was hard stuff. I figured she was due. But I can't say I was at all enjoying this.

When her laughter died out, I asked, "For future reference, what would have been a better question in that situation?"

She got serious for a moment her eyes searching mine. "Honey, 'be my girlfriend' was the exact right thing to say."

"It was?" I asked.

"Yes, it was. Anything more would have been too much. Anything less would not have been enough. It was the perfect thing to say. I'm just saying it was cute."

"Oh," I said, still confused.

She chuckled and said, "You know, that little pout on your face right now is kinda cute."

"Hey!" I said rising, and given how little I was wearing I made sure my posture was good.

"Calm down, my big stud-muffin," she said, holding her hand up. "The thing you need to realize is that cute is good. Cute may not be one step away from getting in bed, but it is only two steps away."

"Two steps?" I asked, making a show of taking two deliberate steps towards her.

"Two steps," she agreed with a smile so hot it could melt an iceberg.

Chapter 26

Taking it Slow
Late Winter 2005, Flagstaff, Arizona

I AM DEBATING WHAT TO SHARE WITH YOU NEXT, HOW MUCH to write. I am calling these missives a "love story" because it is. But there is a limit, that we are fast approaching, to what is appropriate to share. I want to be honest, give you a good taste of what this was like, but not too much.

After a quick stop at the store, I arrived at Licia's door with flowers, wine, and chocolate. It may have been a bit old fashioned, or overkill, but it seemed like the right thing to do.

She opened the door with a thin smile, her hair wet and her face drawn. I was so happy to see her, but at the same time my heart ached to see her so sad.

"Thank you," she said, taking the gifts and ushering me in.

I rubbed my sweating palms on my jeans and took my jacket off. It was winter in Flagstaff, which means it was cold out there.

Her house was small and rustic, nestled on a little cul-de-sac in a development south of town that bordered forest service. Her backyard was a piece of the largest ponderosa pine forest on the continent. The house was small and quaint, very nice. There was a couch in the living room and a bunch of boxes. She hadn't been here long.

"Do the neighbors know who you are?" I asked.

She shook her head. "Not yet. I am actually afraid to unpack. I am afraid one of them will recognize me and the news crews will be camped outside."

I looked around again. The curtains were drawn and not many boxes were unpacked. Not only was she dealing with the trauma of the alien deaths, but with being outed with me by Diane Madison.

"Would you like some tea?" she asked, looking nervous.

"Sure," I answered. It was all painfully awkward.

She made us tea and had me sit on the brown couch while she sat on a chair from the dining room table.

I took a sip of the hot tea and burned my tongue. "You know," I began, "we can take this slow."

She cracked a small smile. "Well, you did say you wanted to be a mess together."

"I did at that," I agreed.

"But," she said, "slow is good."

I don't know what I was expecting, but this wasn't it. I can tell you I wasn't expecting some slow-motion coming together of the romantic comedy couple that have finally admitted they care for each other. I wasn't expecting her to jump right into my arms either. But I certainly wasn't expecting this level of awkward silence and pregnant pauses.

We knew how to interact as q-morphs fighting for the survival of the world. And we had had a nice couple of dates before this "aliens trying to kill us all" thing had gotten serious. But now, things were no longer simple. We were both traumatized, both unsure of the future and our places in it.

"Do you want to talk about it?" I finally asked.

She nodded, biting her lip, and said, "Yeah, but not here."

"THAT'S WHERE HIGHWAY 89A IS," SHE SAID, POINTING to a fold in the land some miles distant. We had gone out her back door and hiked through the pine trees for several miles to get to this place. "And not much farther is Oak Creek Canyon."

I took a deep breath. It was beautiful. Deep canyons in a pine tree forest with a sprinkling of small oak trees, patches of snow in the shadiest spots, cold clean air. We were standing on the edge of a deep cut in the land that sloped down before us. "Nice backyard," I said.

She grabbed my arm and leaned her head on my shoulder. It was just a small, affectionate gesture, but it thrilled me. It was something a girlfriend might do.

"We're going to be okay," I said quietly. I said it to Licia, but I said it to the forest too, and the sky, and the land. It felt still and sacred out here. It felt like if I said things the right way they would have depth and meaning.

"Promise?" she asked quietly.

"I promise," I said, putting my hand on hers as it clutched my bicep.

We stood there for a long time. I could occasionally hear the cars moving along 89A to the south and the west or on I-17 to the east, but otherwise it was silent.

I didn't want to move, I didn't want to break the spell. For in that moment we were okay, just two people falling in love. Our past trauma wasn't relevant in that moment and our future uncertainty was not on our minds. It was Licia and me and the ponderosa pine forest of Flagstaff, Arizona.

It was a blessed point of balance.

It became a touchstone for me. We would come out here often in the coming weeks while we "took it slow," and I would find myself coming out here in my mind when things got stressful (and as you know they got very stressful).

But right then, that moment, everything was fine.

Epilogue

Summer 2025, Casita de Soledad, Central Arizona

I KNOW THAT SOME OF YOU WANT MORE DETAILS. YOU want me to describe those days where we "took it slow" and what happened when we weren't taking it so slow any more. I know some of you want specifics, salacious details. But, sorry, those won't be forthcoming.

I get it, I really do. Two q-morphs whose bodies interact when they come close—what is the sex like? I understand the curiosity, but I will not be satisfying it. I've been married for so long for a reason—there are some lines you don't cross. If you are really curious I suggest you troll the net for some fictional stories of that encounter. I have been told there are many.

But I will leave you with something that I believe is true. The most important ingredient in "making love" is "love." And we were in love. So use your imagination.

LICIA AND I STOOD ON A FLAT PATCH OF HIGH DESERT NEXT to our little greenhouse. She pointed to the pile of building materials and then to a twenty-by-fifteen-foot plot of ground she had cleared of plants and rocks. "So?" she asked.

"Do we really need another greenhouse?" I asked.

"Yes," she replied flatly, her hands on her hips.

I let out an involuntary sigh. Her lips pursed. "It's going to take a while," I said.

She shrugged. "We need to keep busy."

"I guess I'm at a good stopping point with the writing. The boy has got the girl. Peace has come... for a time."

She nodded and then bit her lower lip. "Are you sure you want to keep doing this?"

"Doing what?" I asked.

"Telling our story, the real story. Like you said, it's a good stopping point. People will know a lot more than they did. Maybe it's enough." I paused. It was a good question, and she leapt into that silence. "It is tarnishing your reputation a bit."

"What do you mean?"

"Well, you took credit for defeating the aliens at Yellowstone and it was Toxicwasteman." She held one finger up. "You admitted to being involved with LoVE and robbing that train," she raised another finger. "And the details of our reluctance to harm the aliens will be out in the open if you publish the last one. Do you really want the world to know the 'real' story?"

I paused. On one hand I was irritated, because this line of questioning appeared to be a tool to get me involved in building the new greenhouse. On the other hand I was even more irritated because she had a point.

Our position in the world was no longer what it once was, but what would the world think, what would happen if they knew the truth? If they really saw the full frailty of their heroes?

"It's a fine romantic adventure the way it sits," she said. "Can you let it go?"

"There is so much more to tell," I began, my eyes meeting hers. "While what we have now is a romance, I want to go into what happens after 'happily ever after.' What happens when our hero and heroine hit hard times, what their love looks like as it deepens and grows. And besides, there is the whole war to cover and how we ended up here." I gestured to the parched land around us.

She had been patient these last few months as I wrote. She had supported me and helped deal with the complex emotions that had arisen. Our eyes met and while it was clear she wanted this greenhouse, there was also compassion there. She wanted what she wanted, but it looked to me like she thought I needed a break from rooting around in our past and was smart enough not to come right out and say it.

And she was (as usual) right. Taking an honest look at a tumultuous life is not for the faint of heart. This story is a marathon, not a sprint. There's time for this greenhouse and time to finish the story.

"Okay," I said, and she rewarded me with a smile. "But I want to talk about the future while we do this."

"The future?" she asked.

"Yes, the future. This life we live." I held my arms up and spun around looking at the beautiful, but isolated, place we lived. Rolling hills, wild grasses, prickly pear cactus. "This is our home, our 'fortress of solitude,' but I don't think it's going to be enough for much longer."

She smiled shyly and nodded.

"So," I began, "let's get started."

Want more of the adventures of Neutrinoman and Lightningirl? The following is a sample of Episode #4.

Off Book

Neutrinoman & Lightningirl
A Love Story

Episode #4

Chapter 1

Sarah Speaks

Late Winter 2005, Palo Verde Nuclear Generating Station, Arizona

THE VIDEO WAS GRAINY, BUT CLEAR ENOUGH. IT SHOWED a picture of the alien Sarah dressed in a silver jumpsuit, like when I had rescued her. The classic *The Day the Earth Stood Still* look. She looked good, the cut on her forehead was healing well, her long blond hair was pulled back, her blue eyes intense. The audio was crisp and clear.

This video had been received by mail, sent to Diane Madison at WNN on a little thumb drive. The world hadn't seen it yet, but Diane was going to air it this evening.

Licia, Colonel Williams, General Marcus, Jennifer Johnson, and I were in a hushed little room at the Palo Verde Nuclear Generating Station. A small conference room with a table, chairs, and the video gear. We had been called in with the highest priority, Licia and I driving down from Flagstaff. It was a week after she agreed to be my girlfriend, just twelve days since the Battle at Palo Verde when she quit the program. She only came because Williams asked her personally.

"I am known as Sarah," the tall alien began on the video.

She looked nervous. Behind her was a flat white wall, no clues whatsoever to her location. "I represent the Arcturian Alliance. I am no one, but I will speak for you and all will listen. This is our way."

The room was dead quiet, all eyes fixed on the screen.

"Your planet has been classified as threat. We have been listening and watching you for sixty Earth years. We have been studying you. You are an immature and violent species. The Arcturian Alliance has determined that extermination is required. Several attempts have been made and have failed."

The meteor attack and the "Incident at Yellowstone" came leaping to mind. I wondered if there were others.

"None then spoke on your behalf. I speak now."

General Marcus caught my eye and gave me a small nod. Releasing her had been my idea, and it had caused a major fight between me and the general. This video was starting to sound like Sarah was keeping her end of the bargain. That we did the right thing.

"I have been to your planet. I have witnessed the kindness and compassion of the yellow one. When we fought he saved me. I am no one but he saved me, he saved others, he fought for my release. So now I speak on your behalf and hostilities will stop.

"While I speak, while the council listens and debates, there will be no more attacks by the Arcturian Alliance. This is our way.

"Look in your hearts, people of Earth. Find compassion for one another. Stop your wars and fighting. Stop putting the needs of the individual over the whole. Stop killing each other. This is your chance to change, your one chance. Once

I speak, once they listen, the decision will be final. We will either leave you be or we will destroy you for the sake of all.

"Look to the yellow one. Be more like him.

"I am called Sarah. I am no one, but because of the yellow one, I speak for you."

The video ended and Jennifer turned on the lights. The room was silent, all eyes on me. Colonel Williams rubbed his salt-and-pepper hair and shook his head. General Marcus had this faraway look on his round face. Jennifer just stood there, her arms wrapped around her just like she was cold.

I am the "yellow one" and what Sarah just said made my heart pound hard in my chest. She was asking the world to be more like me. She was holding me up as example. It's too much. I wanted to bolt, to run away. To leave all this behind and just have a normal life with Licia. I didn't want to be the hero.

Under the table, Licia grabbed my hand and squeezed it hard. Her brown eyes were compassionate as she looked at me. Peace had come, but for how long? And if Diane Madison outing me wasn't enough, I now had an alien telling the entire world to stop fighting and to look to me as example.

It was too damn much.

Chapter 2

What Happens in Vegas...
Spring 2005, US-95, Northwest Arizona

I HAVE COME TO KNOW AND UNDERSTAND THE BEAUTY OF the desert. It's not a flashy beauty like the tropics, it's a quiet beauty, deep and abiding, entirely mysterious.

Quinn Rake, my new q-morph partner, drove my 1990 Ford Focus down US-93 in the northwestern corner of Arizona between Kingman and Las Vegas. It's a long lonely stretch of desert with plentiful cactus and craggy hills in the distance.

Spring had come and with it hope. After Sarah's video, the full truth of the alien attacks on our planet had come to light. The governments of the world had even started releasing details they had about previous alien visits: Roswell, New Mexico, in 1947 (it wasn't a weather balloon); the Rendlesham Forest incident in 1980 (alien ships did land in England); Japan Air Lines flight 1628 in 1986 (alien ships seen over Alaska); the Phoenix Lights in 1997 (not airplanes); and more.

I had done more interviews and had become a celebrity. I was dealing with paparazzi when I was out in the world and then with endless training when I was with the military.

This "speaking" Sarah was doing was of an unknown length with a decision making process we couldn't fathom. Everyone was worried the attacks would resume. Just because Sarah implored us to "stop killing each other" and had promised that "we will destroy you for the sake of all" if they perceived the need, didn't mean we could change.

The US was still at war in Iraq and Afghanistan, the Middle East was a disaster, and fighting terrorism was a major pastime here since 9/11. There were no shortages of humans killing humans.

The threat of annihilation often made us less logical, not more.

I stared out at the dirt and sage brush whipping by me. The signs of spring were not overt in the desert, but they were there. Growing green grasses, instead of the usual brown, the lighter green of new growth on the sage brush.

"Are you going to be this pensive the whole trip?" Quinn asked, his blue eyes boring into me as we roared down the two-lane road at ninety miles per hour, the fastest my little Ford could manage.

I looked at him and smiled, but it didn't work very well. I only managed a grimace. As much as I liked Quinn, I finally had some R&R and was spending it with him instead of Licia on our crazy "off book" mission. The military thought we were going to Las Vegas to blow off some steam. In truth we were going there in search of Chaosboy. Since our "little heist" on the train I couldn't stop thinking about him, about how he could bend probabilities with his will, about how he left a wake of chaos and bad luck for others in his wake, about how blasé he was about collateral damage.

An alien threat. Overwhelming celebrity. Chaosboy and the damage he could cause. I had reason to be pensive.

"Because if you going to be big wet blanket, then I think we should turn around now," he said. Quinn had this odd accent that is impossible to place. He said it is because of his Army brat upbringing, spending the first sixteen years of his life in five different countries in Europe, and his French mother.

I took a deep breath and tried to shake it off. Quinn was still staring at me as we roared down the road. It made me nervous, but I understood that it wasn't dangerous for him. Quinn is a q-morph--quantum metamorph--like Licia and I. But unlike us his powers are always present, like Chaosboy and Byte.

During the day the cosmic rays hit, he was working in the Relativistic Heavy Ion Collider in Upton, New York. He was inside the collider inspecting some of the sensors when the collider accidently was triggered. The Collider is a 3.8-kilometer track where ions traveling at relativistic speed (a significant portion of the speed of light) collide so physicists can study the primordial form of matter that existed shortly after the Big Bang. Those particles went through Quinn's body and mixed with those cosmic rays turning him into the q-morph he is today.

He doesn't have a single superhero name like most of us do. Actually he has a lot of superhero names, but no one knows that they all belong to him: The Hammer, Stretchman, Jumper, and others. Actually, he's the reason that most counts of the q-morphs created that day in 2003 are too high. He can control his body at a molecular level and in reality is each of those q-morphs.

And this is why I didn't need to be worried about him looking at me while he was driving down a two-lane highway like a maniac. In his normal form, a handsome and muscular 6'4", he has the best reflexes on the planet and amazing peripheral vision. He could look at me and still drive safely.

But this isn't his natural form. I think it's the body he wanted to have when he was young. He was in his late fifties when the accident happened, but he looks like he's about thirty now.

"Come on, Nik," he said. "We need to have some fun. We've been cooped up for weeks."

"We're going to Vegas for a reason," I said.

"Yes! To gamble and drink and chase women--"

"To find Chaosboy," I said, interrupting. "To stop him."

Quinn was silent, his eyes turning to the road, the smile melting off his face. He ran his right hand through his jet-black hair in a gesture I have come to understand signals nervousness for him. His hair was slicked back and perfect as always. The gesture was completely unnecessary.

"How do you know he is there?" Quinn asked quietly.

I sighed. We had been over this. "Chaosboy has a fan club, a private group on Yahoo. I'm a member."

"And how did you get into group?"

"Byte got me in last month." Byte was Tom Tyree's (aka Toxicwasteman) tech guru. She was a q-morph that could control the Internet with her mind and is part of LoVE (League of Villains Extraordinaire).

"Chaosboy and Byte are both part of LoVE," he said slowly. "Why would she do this thing?"

I shrugged, but I suspected why. There was something Tom and his gang wanted me to do. I knew that Byte had probably run one of her computer simulations, known that evidence of Chaosboy being close might draw me out. I knew that they were probably manipulating me, but that didn't change the fact that I wanted to have a serious conversation with him. That I wanted to bring him in.

The time I spent with LoVE changed me. I no longer doubted that we both had the same goal (eliminate the alien threat, save the world) but it was their methods that disturbed me. I had also come to believe that LoVE was approaching the problem in ways far more innovative than the military.

So maybe this was some convoluted way to get me to do something, but it was in alignment with something I wanted to do. So be it.

"And what will we do with this Chaosboy if we catch him?" Quinn asked.

I stared back out at the desert again, trying to catch more signs of spring, the light green of new growth, the color of a blooming cactus. In truth, I didn't know.

I wanted Chaosboy stopped but how far would I be willing to go to do that?

LICIA DIDN'T KNOW WHAT WE WERE UP TO. SHE THOUGHT we were just out for some fun, some male bonding, cutting loose time. And oddly, she wasn't hurt that I was spending time off without her. Well, that wasn't not odd for her, but odd for other women I have known.

She had been rather withdrawn since she left the program ten weeks ago. At first she tried to go back to her job at Arizona Public Service (APS), but since the world knew who she was and what she looked like, crowds would gather when she was doing dangerous work on high-tension power lines.

She had a fan club, and members of it would roam

Northern Arizona and tell others of her location if they found her. Crowds would gather.

Lately Licia had been holed up in her little cabin backing the forest south of Flagstaff. Taking long walks, wearing a blond wig and dark glasses so her neighbors didn't recognize her, trying to have something of a normal life. But there was no "normal" for us anymore.

"You thinking of her?" Quinn asked. We were past the Hoover Dam and Lake Mead and were headed down towards Boulder City and then Vegas. From here we could see the sprawl of Vegas laid out over the flat desert below.

"Yeah," I said.

"I could help if you like, I could--" he said and I knew what was coming.

"No... please, Quinn. That would just make it..." I trailed off because it was too late. Quinn was morphing, the strange sound of it emanating from his side of the car. It's a disturbingly organic sound: kind of like a cross between flowing water and a cricket chirping. His jet black hair suddenly started growing long, his features changing, his limbs thinning and his body grew shorter. From the bulky 6'4" frame of Quinn Rake to the lithe body of Licia Lopez. Or at least a close enough reproduction to be completely unnerving.

He got the body proportions right, but the face wasn't quite there. The cheekbones were too high, the eyes a bit too big, the lips puffy. And his blue eyes were still there instead of Licia's brown. When Quinn changed, for some reason his eyes didn't.

"Hey, big boy," Quinn-Licia said. "Don't be sad. I am right here." The voice was feminine but definitely not Licia. It takes Quinn a long time to get good at another form. It takes a lot of practice. He wasn't that good at Licia.

"Stop it."

"But hey," she-he said as she-he looked down at her-his chest, "I've always thought these were a little inadequate."

The clicky/squishy sound resumed and Quinn-Licia went from a B-cup to a D-cup, her breasts swelling under the black tank top. "That better. You like?"

I looked away. That weird face, that strange voice, it was just too much. I stared at this abandoned western-themed casino, built to look like an old fort, as we passed it. I didn't want that nightmare version of Licia to stick with me. And for the record, I have never found anything about her physicality to be inadequate.

Quinn's transformation sound started up again for a minute or so. "It's okay now," he said in his normal, deep voice. "Sorry, thought you might find that funny."

"Don't ever do that again," I said, glad to see him back.

He smiled at me, this perfect white-toothed grin. "Of course not."

We drove in silence the rest of the way to the Golden Nugget Casino in old Las Vegas. We knew Chaosboy was there. We had a plan.

Chapter 3

Nabbing Chaosboy
Spring 2005, Las Vegas, Nevada

IN THE CAR SITTING IN THE PARKING GARAGE OF THE Golden Nugget, Quinn started transforming again. The sound always sent a chill down my spine. What he did just wasn't natural. I looked away. I didn't want to witness it.

"It's a little hurtful, you know," he said, his voice feminine and sultry.

"What?" I asked, looking at him. He was now a statuesque blond dressed in heels and a tight red cocktail dress. This was one of his go-to forms he had practiced and was good at. He called her Sadie, so I'll refer to Quinn as this when he is her. (His transformations can certainly challenge the use of pronouns.)

"You are disgusted by who I am," Sadie said, a pouty frown on her face.

I took a deep breath. I couldn't believe he was bringing this up now. Here.

"We are partners now," she said. "We need to embrace each other's unique capabilities." She then pulled up the front of her strapless dress, in a move that is entirely distracting to the heterosexual male. Sadie was well endowed so it was quite the show.

As I tried to come up with something to say I realized that when Quinn turned into Licia earlier and then into Sadie he didn't leave any clothes behind. His clothing as Quinn had been part of his form. Part of him.

"You've been naked this whole time?" I asked. "Seriously, dude? That is not cool."

Sadie shrugged, her blue eyes looking me up and down. The eyes were the one part of Quinn that was still part of Sadie and the lecherous look she/he gave me freaked me out. "Clothing just gets in the way, don't you think?"

I got out of the car and slammed the door. "Oh, hell, Quinn. What is wrong with you?"

Sadie got out of car, her movements slow and sensuous. "Do you know how much fun I can have with this body in a town like this?" Her feminine hands raked up and down her body, the dress leaving little (or just enough) to the imagination.

I sighed. "Just stick to the plan, okay?"

She shrugged and tugged her dress up again. "Chaosboy won't be able to resist me."

Of that there could be no doubt.

MY INTEL PUT CHAOSBOY PLAYING CRAPS IN THE GOLDEN Nugget right now. He was having what he called one of his "Chaos Meets" with a few of his fans. It was basically him showing off to a crowd and raking in lots of money from the casino. His groupies bet with him and made money too.

There were reports of previous versions of this on his Yahoo group. Since they're such a public thing he really had to bend probability hard for the casino to not catch on too soon. Inevitably someone got hurt. A stumble leading to a broken arm in Reno, a fatal heart attack outside of Phoenix, and lots of lots of dropped electronics.

The weird thing was his groupies didn't seem to mind. They seemed to get off on the danger of being near him. This world has no shortage of weirdos.

Our plan was simple. Quinn--or rather Sadie--would go in playing the role of a groupie and lure him away up to her room. Not that we had a room, he was to get Chaosboy to the elevators where I would be waiting.

I had a Bluetooth headset on and was listening through Sadie's phone. She had dialed me once she had spotted him and then stashed the phone (I didn't know where and didn't want to know). The Golden Nugget is a bit of a labyrinth, just like all casinos, and I was hanging out in the south tower lobby at the end of a long hallway that went past the outdoor swimming pool.

"Hey, Red," Sadie said through the phone line. And I do have to admit that she has a wicked sultry voice, a bit Demi Moore, a bit Scarlett Johansson.

"Well, hello there, beautiful," Chaosboy said with his Irish accent. "You're just in time to blow on my dice for luck."

"On this peach of a day," Sadie said. "I'd love to." The phrase "peach of a day" was the code phrase from the Yahoo group. It identified Sadie as one of his core groupies. There was then a very exaggerated blowing sound and a boyish giggle from Chaosboy. I can imagine how Sadie bent over giving him a fine view of her epic cleavage.

No. I don't want to imagine that.

There was a lot of background noise, his cheering groupies,

overlapping conversation, the jangle of slot machines, but I could hear pretty well. I went over to the little Starbucks stand near the elevators and got a coffee. I was nervous, and knew the caffeine probably wouldn't help, but I needed something to divert my attention from Sadie seducing Chaosboy.

Not that it was much of a seduction. I suspect Chaosboy was pretty sure he'd get "lucky" at all of these. He probably didn't even need to bend probability to do it.

I pulled the Red Sox baseball cap low on my head and adjusted my mirror shades. This amounted to my disguise. It wasn't much, but enough. No one recognized me.

There were a few little tables in front of the Starbucks and I took a seat and waited. I listened over the phone to the cheering as Chaosboy had an improbable run at the craps table, as Sadie gushed at his brilliance, as Chaosboy did his occasional boyish giggle.

The coffee was bitter and I drank it slowly. By the time I was down to the cold dregs, the "Chaos Meet" was breaking up and Sadie had convinced Chaosboy to go to her room.

HE WAS TWENTY-ONE, SHORT WITH FLAMING RED HAIR AND green eyes. He was wearing white pants and shirt and a straw hat, the kind of outfit some Florida mobster might wear. Sadie towered over him in her heels. Chaosboy had the biggest damn grin on his face as they walked past the Starbucks to the bank of elevators.

I relaxed a little, it didn't look like he suspected, and he didn't even glance my way while they passed. He was telling her a dirty joke about an Irish priest and a donkey.

After they passed, I tossed my coffee cup in the trash

and ambled towards the elevator. Sadie made a show of bending over to press the up button and Chaosboy took the opening and stared at her ass. I shook my head, the two of them were the pair. Sadie really looked like just the right kind of dumb blond that would go for Chaosboy.

The elevator door dinged, some tourists spilled out before some more got in. Chaosboy made a step towards it but Sadie held him back. "Maybe we can get lucky, Red," she said. "Maybe we can get an elevator to ourselves."

Chaosboy looked her up and down (his head came up to her bosom, so it's more looking them up and down) and grinned. It wasn't long until an empty elevator opened up and they walked in.

I walked in right behind them. Well, I almost didn't. I was positioned properly, only a few steps away, but a guest with a huge trolley of luggage got in between me and the elevator at the last moment. Very unlucky.

Quite ungracefully, I plow right through the middle, spilling their luggage on the floor, and stumbled into the elevator just as it closed.

"Hey, lad," Chaosboy said. "This here is a private party."

"Yes it is," I said, grabbing him by the lapels of his fancy white suit and slamming him against the back of the elevator.

He hit with an "oomph" and then the elevator suddenly stopped as Sadie hit the red emergency stop button. Sadie didn't turn back into Quinn. It was part of the plan, if we could confuse Chaosboy in any way during this it was worth a shot.

I kept him pinned to the back of the elevator with one hand and took off my sunglasses.

"Neutrino!" Chaosboy said. "What is this?"

"It's time for us to have a long talk. A very long talk."

WITH A LITTLE HELP FROM CHAOSBOY, THAT REQUIRED A little coercion from me, we managed to make it to the roof of the Golden Nugget's south tower. It's a flat expanse of dull white with a waist-high wall all around. We were twenty-five stories up in the air and I didn't think it would be easy for Chaosboy to escape us.

Except once we got up there, once the door slammed behind us, once I let go of his neck, his demeanor changed. Radically.

"Well, Neutrino, I'm mighty glad you got my meetin' invite," he said as he strolled across the roof like he was taking a walk on the beach. There was a swagger to his step and a lilt in his voice that made me want to punch him.

"And Quinn," he said, turning to Sadie. "As much as I enjoy ya like this, ya can drop the disguise. We know all about ya, lad."

Sadie looked at me and I nodded. The click-squish sound emanated from him again and soon he was back to Quinn.

It was hot up here, well over a hundred degrees, and I was starting to sweat. "What is this?" Quinn asked, looking at me.

"Chaosboy here," I said, gesturing to the still strutting redhead, "and his gang set this all up. He was expecting us."

"You knew?" Quinn asked.

"I suspected, but it doesn't matter. We can still do what we came here to do."

"Okay, gents," Chaosboy said. "If we're done with pleasantries, let's get down to it." He trotted over to the north edge of the roof that bordered the outdoor ground-level pool and courtyard below and hopped up on the little wall, a big grin on his face.

Quinn rushed over and said, "Don't jump."

I took my time. I wasn't worried about Chaosboy hurting himself. Quinn didn't have much firsthand experience with him yet. Chaosboy was in no danger. I was beginning to doubt that we would be able to contain him, though. I was casting about for a plan when he started talking.

"Your mission, gentlemen," he began in a comical attempt at a deep voice, "should ya decide to accept it, is to stop the q-morph known as Gaia from causing major loss of life in the Las Vegas area and to, if you're able, bring said q-morph onto our side in the battle against the Arcturian Alliance."

He stopped, his hands spread wide, a huge grin on his face. Quinn and I were about five feet away.

Chaosboy pulled a keycard out of his pocket and tossed it to me. "That is for the penthouse suite. Ya have it for the night. A dossier on Gaia is in there--it won't self-destruct or anythin', so don't ya worry. The odds are long on this one, lads," he said, looking at me. "So ya will need your little firefly if you have any chance of capturing Gaia alive." By "little firefly" he was referring to Lightningirl. As I stood there, I hoped to be around when he called her that in person. "There is a plane waiting for her in Flagstaff. Details in the suite."

Quinn and I stood there with our mouths open. In truth I had suspected this as a setup, but not to this degree. A mission? And from the *Mission Impossible* speech it sounded like a hard one. And who the hell was Gaia?

His smile broadened and he looked to Quinn. "If Sadie ever really wants a good time... Well, I'm game."

He took a step back on the wall and looked down before

meeting our gazes again and continued in his not-so-deep voice. "As always, should anyone get caught or killed in this mission, LoVE will disavow any knowledge of your actions."

He got this blank look on his face and then stepped off the wall falling out of sight.

Want more? The next episode of "Neutrinoman and Light-ningirl: A Love Story" will be out soon. To keep abreast of the latest news, sign up for my newsletter at neutrinoman.com (use the yellow box on the right side of the screen).

Acknowledgements

Here we are. It's taken a lot longer to get these done than I had hoped, so thank you for reading along.

And by "here," I mean we've arrived at the point where you can clearly see where this story is going. New superheroes falling in love and trying to save the world. Getting used to powers. Fame. Complicated lives. Doing what must be done while keeping a hold of their humanity.

I'm so happy to be telling this story. There's a ways to go and I'll hope you'll keep following along.

I've had a lot of help getting here.

Many thanks to my super team of beta reader: John Bifano, Roni Hornstein, Chris Kalinich, Michele Lytle, Susanne One Love, and Aleia N. O'Reilly.

Thanks to Diana Cox, my proofreader, for making me look good. (www.novelproofreading.com).

A special nod to my love, my partner, and my wife, Aleia. You *always* inspire me.

Fasten your seat belts, folks. There is a lot more Neutrinoman and Lightningirl coming soon.

About the Author

ROBERT J. MCCARTER IS VERY COMFORTABLE WRITING about characters as long as one of those characters is not himself. Actually, Robert is anything but comfortable speaking (or writing) of himself in the third person—he finds it pretentious and silly.

So, let's drop all that usual bio crap.

Hi, my name is Robert, and I make things up and write them down. As a reader you may be interested in knowing something about me, so here goes:

I am a computer programmer by trade and have been for a very long time. I wrote my first program over thirty years ago and never stopped. I found the dramatic arts in high school, which got me through that rather daunting rite of passage, and fell in love with the arts. After high school, I started writing really bad poetry about how lonely I was and how clueless I was about the opposite sex (which, fortunately for all of us, I burned). After that my writing turned towards fiction.

I have written sporadically for several decades, and in what is, in all probability, part of a mid-life crisis, I started writing seriously (i.e. regularly) a few years ago. I have always been drawn to the arts (acting, photography, fractal art, and writing) and find that I am most happy when I am being as creative as possible. Thus, all the sitting alone at my computer making things up.

My writing is colored by my technical (i.e. geek) past as well as my age. I'm no youngster, so themes of death, grief, and change tend to creep into my writing (Okay, that's an understatement). Also, having been trained as an engineer, I like things to make sense and do my best to keep the hand waving to a minimum.

If you asked me to succinctly say something to summarize my writing style, I would tell you to go buzz off. But then, after profuse apologies, I would say: "I write humanist-geek, character-oriented sci-fi with heart."

I live in the middle of a Ponderosa Pine forest in the mountains of Arizona with my beautiful wife and my ridiculously adorable dog.

If you'd like to get a hold of me, use the contact form on my website (RobertJMcCarter.com/contact-me/). I'd love to hear from you, really I would.

Oh, and if you want the inside scoop on my writing, sign up for my newsletter (I won't share your name and emails are infrequent—around once a month). You can sign up using the blue box on the right of my website at RobertJMc-Carter.com.

Also by Robert J. McCarter

Novels in the "Ghost's Memoir" world:
Shuffled Off: A Ghost's Memoir, Book 1
Drawing the Dead
To Be a Fool: A Ghost's Memoir, Book 2

Novellas (short novels) in the
Neutrinoman and Lightningirl Series:
Meteor Attack!
   Lightningirl and Neutrinoman, A Love Story. Episode 1
Toxic Asset
   Lightningirl and Neutrinoman, A Love Story. Episode 2
Protocol X
   Lightningirl and Neutrinoman, A Love Story. Episode 3
Off Book
   Lightningirl and Neutrinoman, A Love Story. Episode 4
   (Coming soon)

Novelettes
Probability: Resolve
The Turing Test Will Be Televised
Ghost Hacker, Zombie Maker